THE SWAN DRESS MURDERS

COZY CRAFT
BOOK 4

MILLIE RAVENSWORTH

1

Izzy was light-headed from blowing up balloons.

"There are pumps for blowing up balloons," she pointed out. "Why are we doing it the old-fashioned way?"

"We should all be more environmentally-conscious," replied Olivia, with a prim glance at Izzy. "A balloon pump is just another thing we can easily make do *without* if we try."

From what they'd been discussing Izzy had the distinct impression that, if she had her way, Olivia would make society do away with all sorts of things, like shoes and chocolate, so she let it go. The minimalist interior of the wooden lodge was being steadily covered with gaudy plastic decorations, but neither Izzy or Olivia were in charge of the overall event so they just kept up their gentle balloon-based bickering.

That was the thing with hen parties. You had to be

friendly with people who weren't necessarily your friends. The bride was the only one who really knew everybody.

The bride on this occasion was Briony Hart, or *'Bri the Bride'* as the balloons declared.

Izzy was Olivia's cousin, but they did not socialise. Izzy would occasionally see Olivia in town buying vegan pasties from one of the stalls in Framlingham market, but Olivia would never pop into the Cozy Craft shop to say hello. Both of them were fine with being distant cousins, because both of them knew that they moved in very different circles. Olivia's circle was probably a perfect sphere of zen-like calm, where everyone sat around sipping herbal tea, while Izzy's circle was probably shaped more like a pretzel or maybe even a helter-skelter. The only time Izzy had seen Olivia recently was for their grandma's birthday party, where there had been some weird expectation that Izzy, as the dressmaker, would provide fancy dress outfits for free. That assumption had been gently fixed (as evidenced by a complex family discount poster Izzy kept to hand in the dressmaking shop) which went some way towards explaining Olivia's current brittle attitude.

The two of them had been put on balloon blowing duty as they had arrived early. They were all staying in fancy alpine lodges in the grounds of Letheringham Hall. There was nothing remotely alpine about Letheringham Hall or the local area — the county of Suffolk rarely saw snow, even now in the middle of winter, and it certainly had no mountains. Suffolk's beautiful countryside was like a ruffled bedspread, full of unexpected folds and hollows, sprinkled with isolated villages and the odd herd of deer, but no mountains.

The main building of Letheringham Hall, once a stately home and now a classy hotel, would serve as the wedding venue in three weeks' time when Briony Hart would marry Ross Blowers. The much newer guest lodges were a distance away down the hill, near the woods and the lake. The bridal lodge was the largest, and was where the selected guests would spend the evening ensuring Briony had a wonderful time celebrating her upcoming wedding and her last days of freedom.

They were in a large luxurious lounge inside the lodge, with a sectional sofa that would seat at least six people, and several easy chairs. There were low tables for drinks, and some larger tables off to the sides.

The other guests were now beginning to drift in. Olivia went over to greet them. Izzy recognised a tall and broad hipped figure amongst the new chattering arrivals.

"Oh hi, Monica!" She waved.

Izzy had met Monica during the car show in the town the previous summer. Amongst the classic cars that had filled the town that weekend, Monica and her friends had their own little enclave of much-loved Land Rover off-road vehicles.

Monica gave Izzy a brief quizzical frown, smiled as she remembered who she was (or perhaps just pretended to) and came over to help with the balloons.

"Thank God, a familiar face," said Monica.

"How do you know Briony?" asked Izzy.

"She's marrying my brother," said Monica.

"Oh," said Izzy, who knew almost nothing about Ross Blowers. "So, Briony's future sister-in-law. You'll be part of the Hart family or, rather, she'll become a Blower."

"Blowers, yes. Lucky us. Briony seems nice, although," Monica lowered her voice, "she doesn't drive, did you know that?"

Izzy laughed. Monica's life, as far as she knew, revolved around her beloved Land Rovers to such an extent that her fellow 'Sufflanders', as they called themselves, were definitely her real family. Looking back at the women gathered round Briony at the door, Izzy could see how Monica would want to latch onto Izzy at this event. There was a certain type to several of the women — slender, blonde, not too tall, not too short. Monica failed to hit the mark on all counts.

Izzy spotted an older woman, equally blonde, equally trim, among the hen party. "So your brother is going to have Shirley as a mother-in-law?" she said.

Monica smiled, knowingly. "Oh yes. But our Ross is a farmer. Thick-skinned, thick-headed and made of stern stuff. He will be fine."

There was a tap on the door of the party lodge. The nearest woman, Catriona Wallerton, opened it. Cat had the cake shop on Market Hill. Izzy had known her for many years, and still popped into the shop several times a week for a restorative sausage roll or a cakey treat.

"Strip-o-gram!" Cat declared loudly.

"Shush!" said mother-of-the-bride Shirley. "It's only hotel staff."

The man had a long tombstone face but a friendly, eager-to-please smile. "Good evening, ladies. I just wanted to check in and make sure that that everyone has access to their rooms."

"This is James Coombes, everybody," said Briony. "He's the events manager here. Sorting out our wedding day too."

Izzy vaguely recognised James as a face she'd seen about town. A friend of a friend, perhaps.

"I need to go and find my lodge," said Cat.

James handed them their keys. "Miss Wallerton. Er, Miss Upton. Olivia. Ah, Miss King. You will find that your names are on the doors, so you shouldn't have a problem finding your rooms. There are paths between all of the lodges. After dark, there are little solar lights along the paths and, if you have to come back up to the main hall, security lights come on to light the way. It does get dark in the countryside."

This was probably something he had to say frequently, for the benefit of any city dwellers who came to Letheringham Hall. Used to constant streetlamps and the orange glow of light pollution, plenty of visitors to the countryside remarked on how dark the nights actually were, especially in the depths of winter.

"Stay on the paths while it's dark," advised James. "We don't want you stumbling into the lake."

"Lake?" said Cat.

"Mmmm," said James, and pointed away, through the wall. "Down the hill. Call it a lake, call it a pond. There's a nice walk round it. Various fish. Some ducks and swans. We've just poured the foundation footings for a wind turbine out on the central island. Green energy. Very environmentally conscious here at Letheringham."

Olivia nodded in the noisy and approving manner of someone who wanted others to see she approved. James smiled at her.

"James, could you uncover some of the food on the side table?" asked Shirley with a regal wave.

Izzy caught the look on James's face. It was a look that said an events manager was not the same as a personal butler, but he smiled nevertheless, and went over to do Shirley's bidding.

As James passed one of the tables he paused and picked up a packet of drawing pins. "Just checking you won't be using drawing pins on the wall in here? I can fetch you some blu tack as an alternative if you would like?"

"But we're all going to play 'pin the tail on Brad Pitt' later on," said Shirley, as if that was explanation enough.

Olivia held up a hand. "Don't worry, James. I'll make sure we don't damage anything."

James looked as if he wanted to say more, but instead just gave Olivia a grateful look and went back to uncovering the food.

Izzy collected her bags from the door and, key in hand, went out with others in search of her little lodge. The lodges were like cute little pretend hobbit houses, Izzy thought, and everything inside them was geared around being comfortable and having fun, with no dreary clutter like mops or vacuum cleaners to remind you of real life.

"Your veranda faces the rising sun," Olivia said to Cat.

"Is that important?"

"Perfect for a yoga practice. Sun salutations with the rising sun."

Cat scoffed. "Don't think I'm going to saluting the rising sun in the morning. I'm going to sleep like the dead until the chambermaid turfs me out."

Izzy peeled off along her own little path to her own little lodge. Time to drop off her bags and let the party begin.

2

In the party lodge, Shirley clapped her hands and loudly declared, "Everybody! Let me tell you about our schedule for this evening."

Shirley was now immaculate in a sparkling emerald green evening dress and high strappy heels, which made her tower over everybody, although the pile of the shaggy rugs dotted around on the floor was causing her some difficulty.

"First of all, we will charge our glasses with some fizz and then I thought we might have an impromptu fashion show, so we can talk each other through our outfit choices for this evening. Would that be fun?"

Shirley was clearly not seeking actual feedback, or she might have caught the look of puzzled dismay on Monica's face.

"After that we have some games planned, and of course lots of drinks and nibbles on hand. You'll see that there is a photo collage on the wall featuring our beautiful bride through the years."

Shirley waved an imperious hand at the far wall, which featured a huge assortment of photographs.

"Are there pictures of us?" said Cat.

As the guests gravitated towards the collage, Izzy recognised her GP among the group. "Ooh, hello, Doctor Upton," she said. Izzy was vaguely aware that she and Denise Upton had been at school together but, as with Olivia, they did not share the same social circles. Izzy would have to reflect later on whether her own crazy circle had ever intersected with anyone else's at all.

"Oh goodness, Izzy King. Call me Denise."

"I can try. Promise me it won't get weird next time I have a smear test?"

Denise laughed. "As long as you promise me that you won't produce a hidden rash for me to look at when you've had a few drinks."

"I'm sure nobody would do that."

Denise gave her a more serious, weary look.

"Care to place money on that? Now, I've mentioned drinks but my hand seems to be empty."

She turned away to seek out a bottle of fizz, leaving the others to coo over the photographs on the wall.

Izzy wondered how it was possible for Denise Upton to retain such a fresh face when she spent her life looking at tonsils and toenails. Maybe doctoring was truly a vocation, a labour of love.

The wall of photographs was utterly absorbing. Izzy

realised that she was doing an initial scan to see if she was in any of them. No doubt everyone else was doing the same thing. Izzy spotted some outfits she had made back in the day. Bittersweet memories, as not everything had turned out as she'd hoped. She snapped a couple of pictures with her phone.

"Oh Briony, you've always been so smiley!" said Olivia, pointing at a toothy preschooler with pigtails in her hair.

"In spite of the hairstyle," added Briony, raising her glass and eyeing her mother.

"Don't even think about laying that at my door," said Shirley. "It was all you really cared about at that age, which bobbles you wanted in your hair, and woe betide me if they didn't match!"

There was a school picture that included Briony, Olivia, Izzy, Cat and Denise within a densely-packed cluster of bodies, some sitting on chairs, some standing and others on a bench at the back.

"Oh, I look so goofy with my retainer," said Cat with a delicate pout at her young self.

With a glass of fizz in her hand, Izzy felt slightly more kinship with her fellow hens. Besides Izzy herself, there were six of them in the lodge — Briony the bride, Olivia, Cat, Doctor Denise, Sufflander Monica and mother-of-the-bride Shirley. Together the seven of them were making enough noise for twenty, but that was the alcohol and the joy of frivolous fun.

"Fashion show time!" said Shirley, clucking over them like a diamante-sprinkled mother hen. "We'll keep it light of course, but everyone please talk us through what you're wearing and what it says about you. I'll put some suitable tunes on."

Shirley laid out a catwalk on the carpet using two strings of fairy lights, while everyone took a seat.

"I don't mind going first," said Cat. She scampered up from the sofa and stood at the start of the catwalk, pausing to flick out her skirt and perform a slight turn. She walked slowly along between the fairy lights. "My outfit today is a figure-hugging sweater dress in the ginger colour that we've all been told is *de rigeur* this season. I mainly bought it to go with these gorgeous vintage style wedge-heeled shoes." She turned and gave a heel kick. "Aren't they to die for? They're four inches high but so very comfy I could walk for miles."

"Your doctor might disagree on that," Denise murmured into her glass.

Izzy had to agree with Cat about the beautiful shoes. They had wide swirled stripes of ginger and petrol blue which ran from the toe up the massive wedge of the heel for maximum impact.

"My necklace matches the blue on the shoes," continued Cat. "It is, of course, Mexican turquoise set in silver, a statement piece."

"Lovely, thank you, Cat," said Shirley. "Next?"

Olivia trotted to the end of the catwalk. "I'm wearing an ethically sourced but individually tailored babycord dress decorated with Sangria-coloured poppies. Simple and classic."

Izzy wondered why Olivia would describe poppies as

Sangria-coloured, but decided not to ask. Instead, she pushed herself to her feet, suddenly feeling three glasses of prosecco run to her legs.

"I can share Izzy's wardrobe choices for today if you'd like?" she said.

She made her way to the catwalk, and deliberately walked on the outside of it. "Izzy is today modelling the trousers that she loved as they were, but unfortunately the hem got snarled in her bicycle, which is why she came up with the novel idea of knitting a colourful insert for the bottom. She was inspired by her recent work on a pair of Elvis trousers, and decided that gored inserts were a lot of fun. Izzy's top is a viscose blouse featuring a cartoon strip print and a jumper because she thought it looked a bit chilly out. In her spare time, Izzy likes to play percussion instruments and talk about herself in the third person."

Izzy sat back down, mostly missing her seat. She'd hoped for more laughs, to break the weird competitive vibe that this fashion show seemed to be generating.

However, perhaps inspired by her off-beat performance, Monica bounded up. "Monica is wearing her ex-army trousers because that is mostly what she always wears."

"Very macho," Cat noted.

"They're very practical and are also cheap as chips. Monica's top is a Sufflanders hoodie. Note the eighty-three Land Rover Defender printed on the back. Monica owns several of these hoodies, as the Sufflanders needed to make up the minimum order."

Monica minced up and down, showing off the hood and

its drawstring by pulling it tight round her face for comic effect.

Izzy laughed. "Good job!"

Shirley smiled politely, but Izzy thought she looked unamused. "Denise?"

"On it!" said Denise and trotted forward. "Denise will also refer to herself in the third person, because she has no real clue as to why her outfit is in any way significant. In fact, she doesn't even know what this is."

"It's a shirtwaister dress made from an autumnal plaid," offered Izzy.

"That's good to know," said Denise. "Now can anyone tell us what it says about Denise?"

Briony chipped in. "She's a hard-working doctor who doesn't waste time on frivolities, but still looks low-key fabulous."

Denise took a bow and sat down. Izzy wanted to applaud her for gently mocking this terrible activity, but still somehow being adored by everyone. Maybe that was a skill she'd picked up at doctor school.

"I'm last!" trilled Shirley. "An old broad, but I can still be fabulous, can't I?"

She twirled her way up the catwalk. "My outfit is sourced from the Dress Agency in Wickham Market."

Izzy resisted the urge to roll her eyes. She knew the Dress Agency and its owner, Carmella Mountjoy, and had little time for the woman's elitist attitudes towards fashion.

"It's a Roberto Cavalli from the early noughties," said Shirley. "I chose it for the striking colour. My eyes are a very close match to this colour if you look at them through a green filter. Fascinating, isn't it? Carmella showed me that. She's such a genius."

Monica leaned over to whisper in Izzy's ear. "Doesn't everything look green through a green filter?"

"Yes, it does, Monica," Izzy agreed.

3

Penny Slipper, sitting in the corner of a pub bar, felt her phone buzz. It was a message from Izzy.

Carmella has convinced Bri's mum to buy a green dress because it matches her eyes if you look at them through a green filter.

Penny tapped an immediate reply.

Don't everyone's eyes look green through a green filter?

I know!

Tragic. Enjoy! Penny sent and put her phone away.

"Sorry," she said to Oscar. The pub was crowded and noisy with chatter, but Penny didn't care. She was ensconced in her own little corner of the Crown Hotel, just across from her own sewing shop, with a glowing open fire just to one side, one of her favourite men beside her and the most delightful present laid out in front of her.

"Oscar, this has to be one of the nicest things that anyone has ever done for me."

Oscar Connelly was freshly back from his work trip to New York. He worked for a fabric wholesaler in London, and Penny had missed him while he'd been away, even though their relationship had not yet moved beyond dinner dates and mostly hypothetical plans for weekends away. He had just presented Penny with a scrapbook, an actual physical old-time scrapbook that she held in her hands. Each page that she turned over was delightful in a new way.

"You've got actual printouts of photos in here."

"It's better than that. Do you know what a Polaroid is?" Oscar asked.

"I'm not *that* young," she laughed. "An instant picture camera thing."

"Yep, well I took one of those around with me. It's quite the conversation-starter. People will pose for a picture with one of those when they wouldn't give you the time of day with your phone camera. Plus it meant that I could work on the scrapbook while it was still fresh in my mind."

Penny ran a finger down the fabric samples fixed to the page, and saw how they related to the stores or garments in the pictures.

"It's incredible."

She was referring not only to the scrapbook itself, but also to the idea that Oscar had carried this around with him on his trip and worked on it constantly. It spoke of a level of care that took her breath away. She sipped her wine to distract herself from the fact that her eyes had filled with tears.

"You must have been so busy on your trip, and yet you took the time to do this for me."

Oscar nodded. "I had to do it, because it was eating away at me. I realised almost immediately. Every cool new thing I saw in the garment district, all I could think about was how much I wanted to share it with you."

"Garment district, it sounds incredible." Penny had heard the words but now, with the pictures and samples, she was beginning to understand the reality of so many specialist businesses packed into a single area. She stabbed a picture with a finger. "Buttonholes while you wait? Seriously?"

"Yep!" Oscar grinned. "Dollar a piece and they just put them on your garment right there."

"I hear a lot of customers complain that they avoid working on things with buttonholes because they hate making them so much."

"Yeah, I hear that too. With a dedicated machine and someone whose job it is to make them all day long, you can see how this has caught on."

"I can."

Oscar turned to a fresh page. "Mood is one of the most famous fabric shops in the world. That's partly because it's been on a TV programme called Project Runway, and partly because it carries such a comprehensive stock."

Penny felt some of the samples and read the description. "Linen twill with metallic gold highlights. It's gorgeous, I've never seen anything quite like this." It was a putty colour with a pale blue stripe. The metallic element was there as a subtle accent, and Penny could picture some dashing summer trousers made from it.

"So many of their fabrics are like that," said Oscar, "unusual, niche and simply fabulous. You could spend hours browsing, or you could go in there with a plan and find the exact thing you need without fear of disappointment."

"It sounds amazing."

"Oh! And they have a shop dog! His name is Swatch."

Penny poured more wine. "We need a drinking game for this. I have to take a swig every time you knock me sideways with another anecdote."

"Are you sure you don't need to get back for your own shop dog at some point?"

Oscar was sadly right. Monty the corgi shared the shop space with Penny and Izzy and, particularly as the nights grew colder, shared Penny's bedroom with her in the flat above.

"He's a big boy. I can stay out for one more. But just one. Izzy will probably have a monster hangover in the morning. I don't want to compete."

Oscar's expression was quizzical, interested.

"Oh, she's at a hen do. This place called Letheringham Hall just south of Fram. Stuck out in these luxury isolated lodges with a bunch of champagne-fuelled giggling old school friends."

"Sounds lovely," said Oscar.

"Oh, I think I'd rather die," said Penny and turned over another page in the scrapbook.

4

"Is it time for Pin the Tail on Brad Pitt?" said Cat.

"Not quite yet," said Shirley, "first of all we're playing *Would you Rather?*"

Briony shrugged. "Would I rather what?"

Shirley grinned. "Exactly. I read each of you one of these questions. You'll soon see. She picked up her printed list. "Who wants to go first?"

"I will!" said Monica.

"Good! Here's the first question on the list Monica. Would you rather ... have a really bad haircut or go bald?"

"Huh. Haircut," mused Monica. "Had some doozies in my time. Especially when I did it myself."

"No way!" said Cat. "I could never dare to do that. You're not so fussy about such things though are you, Monica?"

"Er, I guess not?"

"It's so nice to be a woman who doesn't care about her appearance."

Monica adjusted her hoodie uncomfortably.

"Oh, I'm sure there's a beautiful swan under there somewhere, dear," Cat laughed.

"Give me a question," said Olivia.

Izzy tapped Monica on the shoulder and offered to top up her wine. In the face of insensitive idiots, a bit of comfort and wine were always helpful. Izzy had let Catriona Wallerton generally slip from her social life over the years and was only now remembering why that had been such an easy thing to do.

"Olivia, would you rather … hear pleasant lies or ugly truths?" said Shirley.

"Oof, that's easy. Give it to me straight and honest."

"Honesty is always the best policy," added Doctor Denise, raising her glass.

"And give me a man who can make a bloody decision or give an opinion," said Olivia.

"But you have a man," said Cat, pointedly.

"And Gavin will just beat around the bush rather than show any decisiveness," said Olivia, which drew some drunken laughs.

"Well, he's been an absolute wizard with the floral displays for the wedding," said Briony.

Olivia swung her wine glass at Briony in slightly drunken agreement. "Yep. Great florist, but dating him is like playing hide and seek or something. I want a man to be up front with me, you know? I was only saying the other day that I want a man who'll come up to me and tell me that he's crazy about me and can't live without me. You know, come swooping in with a box of chocolates like that... that one in the old adverts."

"The man from Del Monte," said Shirley.

Briony laughed. "That's not the one, Mum."

"No. Oh, no. He's the one with the tinned fruit."

"Fruit. Chocolates. I don't care. Just give me that man," said Olivia.

"A question for the bride now!" said Cat.

Shirley consulted the list. "Here we go, would you rather...lose all of your friends but keep your BFF *or* lose your BFF and keep the rest of your friends?" Shirley looked up. "BFF means Best Friend Forever if you were —"

"—Yeah we know Mum! Wow, that's a stinker!" Briony protested.

"Not about to abandon your best friend?" asked Cat, her hands pressed to her chest in mock horror.

Briony swayed a little as she wrinkled her brow in thought. "Well, I'm not sure that someone can just *decide* they're your BFF."

"I think you'll find I wrote that on your cast when you broke your leg when you were sixteen," said Cat.

"That's like legally binding," Denise nodded.

"From a 'BFF' who was probably fifty percent responsible for the broken leg in the first place," Briony reminded her.

"Hey, I'm not the guy plying you with cheap cider that night," said Cat. "Also, only a BFF would do your wedding cake at mate's rates," she added. "Oh, tonight's food, like the wedding cake, is courtesy of Wallerton's. All made by my fair hands."

She gestured at the food on the side and Izzy realised she'd been drinking on an empty stomach for over an hour.

"I'm hungry," said Izzy, getting up.

"Classic greedy guts Izzy," said Cat. "Do try the cornbread over there. I made it myself and it's fantastic with dips."

"Is it all vegan?" asked Olivia.

"Stay clear of the butter pastries but everything else is animal-free."

Izzy tucked in. Cat was correct in that the cornbread was the perfect vehicle for consuming dips. She dunked and slathered her way through the selection, while Shirley mixed some cocktails.

"This cornbread is really something Cat," said Olivia.

Cat smirked. "Secret ingredient. I always save the fat that I pour off the pan when I cook bacon. It adds a certain tasty zing to things like this," said Cat.

"Bacon?" said Olivia, the colour draining from her face. "You told me it was vegan."

Cat's face froze. It was clear she now realised she had earlier spoken in error. She tried to compose herself but not quickly enough.

"Well, it is really, when you think about it," Cat said. "It's not the bacon itself, it's just the drippings. You said yourself it's delicious, so it looks like your tastebuds needed it."

Olivia dashed from the lodge. Izzy understood how she felt. There was a level of trust that you put in people when it came to ingredients, especially someone who was a professional baker.

"Jesus, Cat!" said Briony.

Cat bridled. "What? A moment ago everyone loved it!"

"I don't see the fuss," said Shirley. "The pig wasn't killed to make that cornbread. A lot of this vegan business is a cry for attention."

"Oh, Mum!" said Briony.

"Maybe you'll need an ingredients warning on your wedding cake," said Denise, with a light-heartedness that the moment didn't deserve and which she wouldn't have shown if she wasn't more than a little drunk.

There came the sound of retching from outside.

"Oh, she's sick now," said Shirley and it seemed everyone immediately looked to Denise, the local doctor.

"You can't have an allergic reaction to traces of bacon fat," said Denise. "Probably."

"I will go to her," said Cat, with a solemnity that both acknowledged this was her fault, and also made it clear she was being the bigger person by going to assist Olivia.

She pushed herself up, tottered only momentarily on her wedge heels and walked out. The women in the lodge were quiet, listening out, and then came Cat's muffled voice.

"Come on. Come back here! Where are you going to go? Bridesmaids stick together."

Through the gauzy curtain a powerful white light was suddenly visible. The security lights on the path leading up to the main Letheringham Hall building.

Briony looked round at her four remaining hen party guests.

"Well, this party's a bust, isn't it?"

"Are you kidding?" said Denise. "Let's crack open another bottle of fizz and bitch about Catriona. The stories I could tell you..."

"Ever since you were kids, that girl always did have a thoughtless streak," said Shirley. "Called poor Monica an ugly duckling earlier."

"Did she?" said Monica, surprised.

"Something like that."

"*Alternatively*," Izzy said loudly, cutting through the bitter words, "we could play Shirley's Pin the Tail on Brad Pitt game."

Shirley scoffed. "You heard the man. No drawing pins."

"So what about a food-based alternative?"

"Eh?"

Izzy demonstrated. "Here. I break the tip off a bread stick, like this." She held it aloft. "Then I daub the base with a suitable dip, like hummus, and I can play the game." She held a hand over her eyes to demonstrate that she was playing blindfold. "You guide me towards your picture of Brad Pitt and I put the tail where I think it should be. Although it wants to be on a table and not on the wall or this really will end badly."

Shirley gave a lewd chuckle. "Are you suggesting that the winner then gets to eat the results?"

Izzy shrugged. "I wasn't, but that is for the winner to decide."

"You know Brad Pitt is old enough to be my dad, don't you Mum?" said Briony.

"You should be so lucky," Shirley tutted.

Monica waggled her length of breadstick and frowned. "This isn't meant to be an actual tail at all, is it?"

Shirley gave her a wink. "This is a hen party. Had you forgotten?"

A considerable time later, when the picture of Brad Pitt had been obliterated beneath a mess of breadsticks, French onion dip, hummus and guacamole, the door to the lodge opened and Cat and Olivia came back in, arm in arm. Olivia looked very queasy, but she gave a watery smile as she took her seat. Cat was grinning like the cat that had got the cream.

"All sorted and mended," said Cat. She regarded the destroyed Brad Pitt with a superior gaze. "Had fun in here, girls?"

The collected group of women simply looked at her.

Cat snagged an unopened bottle of fizz from the side and ripped off the foil top. "I see a lot of empty glasses in here. Time to take this party to the next level."

5

Izzy woke in the morning with a thick head. It was still very dark, so she hugged the soft pillow and napped for a short while longer, enjoying the feel of high quality cotton sheets. Eventually, she prised herself out of bed to get a drink of water. Her own little pine lodge had a bedroom, a bathroom and a little lounge/dining area that led onto the veranda. Everything was within three strides of everything else but it still took her several minutes to fumble to the bathroom, find a glass and pour a drink.

Of course, the act of moving around had given strength to her headache and she felt that a paracetamol tablet or two would be needed soon enough.

She had no idea what time they'd actually called it quits the night before. It was probably some time after they'd drained the last bottle of prosecco. With the exceptions of Briony and Shirley who were sharing the big lodge, they'd each wended their way down their little paths to their individual lodges, breath misting in the frigid winter air. Cat had battled with her door for a considerable time before loudly slamming it shut behind her. Izzy had been drunkenly working her way towards her bed when a powerful security light came on outside, shining directly into her room through the thin curtains, as if she were about to receive a visitation from angels.

"Hell's Bells!" she had shouted loudly and, from outside, Monica had replied with an apology.

Izzy had gone to sleep thinking that no one else had better be setting off the lights in the night and, despite the tossing and turning and general light sleeping she always suffered from when she'd had too much to drink, had slept through to morning.

The card in Izzy's lounge told her that a luxury breakfast would be served in the hotel from seven, and — she determined, looking blearily at the time on her phone — that was only half an hour away. She dressed in comfortable jeans and a baggy jumper, and wandered out. A white mist hung around the lodges, deadening the colour of the surrounding woods and deepening the profound silence of the place.

She decided that a slow, cool, cleansing walk up to the hotel might just do her some good.

"Ready to greet the dawn?"

Izzy turned in surprise. Olivia sat in a loose yoga pose on her veranda. She was under-dressed for the time of year but seemed entirely comfortable.

"Up early," Izzy managed to say.

"The sun does not rise according to our timetable,"

pronounced Olivia chirpily, drawing a line with her hand to the place where the sun might be hidden behind all the cloud and mist. Olivia seemed absolutely none the worse for a night of drinking and silliness.

"Gonna get some breakfast," said Izzy, who didn't think her brain could handle either yoga poses or Olivia's cheeriness.

She made her way up the defined path towards the hotel proper. As she passed the last of the lodges she noticed something on the path. It was a shoe, one of the fancy wedge heels that Cat had been wearing.

Izzy brushed the dew off the suede with a tut. It would be spoiled if it got water stained.

Some sort of bird screeched in the middle distance.

"Super drunk, Cat," Izzy murmured to no one, and set the shoe on a bench nearby where, if it wasn't spotted by someone else, she could collect it on her return.

Letheringham Hall emerged slowly from the morning mist. It had almost certainly never served as a defensive castle, but it still had little crenelations and ornamental towers along its high roof. It was grand, imposing, and with its terrace and commanding view over the sloping fields, would be a delightful wedding venue for Briony and Ross.

In the hotel restaurant, which might well have been a ballroom in decades past, the bride and the mother of the bride were already seated.

Shirley, dressed this morning in a more subdued outfit of a crimson wraparound blouse paired with palazzo pants, took one look at Izzy and said, "My poor dear, I suspect you won't be the only one with a headache today. I've got some painkillers in my bag, but if you'd like to go for hair of the dog I believe they have Buck's Fizz and Bloody Marys on offer."

Izzy decided that a pill and some orange juice might be best. She would eat in a bit when her head had stopped swimming. She sat down and gladly accepted coffee when the smart young waitress offered it.

Over the next half hour, Denise, Monica and Olivia appeared, none of them looking as delicate as Izzy felt. Perhaps Olivia's yoga and veganism offered some armour against the demon drink. Perhaps there was something genetic in Monica's farming stock that had inured her against long nights. And Denise… Izzy gave a mental shrug. Perhaps the doctor had filled her overnight bag with better pills than the rest of them had access to.

"The buffet awaits," said Shirley.

"Cat's not here," pointed out Olivia.

"She'll come," said Briony. "You can never shake Cat off for long."

Some moving more eagerly than others, the group approached the long line of tureens, platters and baskets that held the hotel's breakfast offering. Monica gave herself double helpings of bacon and sausage.

"Pigs is made for eating," she whispered to Izzy when she was sure Olivia wasn't in earshot.

Izzy was drawn to a selection of delicious-looking pastries — croissants, pain au chocolat, cinnamon rolls, jam filled turnovers. She took several, together with a handful of strawberries in the instinctive belief that a bit of fruit might counteract the bad calories in the pastries.

By her second coffee, Izzy was feeling much more human, and the conversation was more relaxed than it had been the night before. Olivia was telling Monica about the floral arrangements her boyfriend was doing for the wedding itself.

"Cat's cake and Gavin's flowers, it's mates' rates all round for your wedding," Denise noted.

"No expense is being spared," Shirley was keen to point out, "but we recognise local talent when it's there to be used. Briony only got this place thanks to old friendships."

As if by magic, James the events manager was at their table, a smile bringing life to his tired and funereal face.

"Did we all sleep well?" he asked, hands clasped together.

"Very well, young man," said Shirley and there were happy murmurs of agreement.

"Cat's still not here," said Olivia.

"She's going to miss out on breakfast," said Denise. "Most important meal of the day. Or top three at least."

"She's probably hungover," said Izzy. "I found her shoe."

"What?" asked Briony.

"On the path on the way over here."

"On the path?"

"You don't mean on the island?" said Monica.

Izzy frowned. "Why would I mean on the island?"

"I thought I saw..." Monica paused and dabbed at some ketchup on her chin. "I was taking a walk down by the lake and thought I saw it."

"The lake? The path? Where has that woman been in the night?" said Denise, eyes sparkling mischievously.

There was an amused titter from a some of the group, but

Izzy resolved to take a walk back after breakfast and see if she could find these widely cast shoes.

With almost psychic insight, Monica hurried to catch up with Izzy as she walked down the path back towards the lodges, and asked, "Want me to show you where the shoe was?"

"Yes, if you don't mind."

The lake was on the far side of the lodges, and on the path down they walked past the bench where Izzy had left the shoe. The shoe had gone. It was definitely the only bench, and the shoe wasn't there.

"It's gone," Izzy said.

"I guess that means Cat's up already and taken it."

"I suppose."

They wandered on.

The low winter sun had driven away the mist, and now the view of long lawns leading to forested hollows was quite beautiful.

"Is it very wrong of me," said Monica "that I can't look at a nice garden like this without imagining driving the Landie over it?"

Izzy laughed. "You would probably not be popular, although it would be quite a spectacle."

The lodges were arranged in a tight circle, like a cute little village. The path in from the hotel became the path out towards the lake.

"I took a walk down here before breakfast," said Monica. "Thought I'd get a look at the wind turbine. The hotel says it's gonna be carbon neutral by the end of the next year. The wind turbine'll provide power to a microgrid for the entire complex."

"You big into green energy?" asked Izzy, mildly surprised.

"Saving money, saving the planet," Monica shrugged. "Just makes sense."

Through the dense little woodland, they came out on the banks of what Izzy would have described as a large fishing pond, picturesque enough but not perhaps of sufficient size to be called a lake.

"The wind turbine will be over there," said Monica, pointing.

Out in the middle of the grey waters, past the gathered waterfowl, was what looked like a small grassy island. It was surrounded by orange plastic fencing, and there was a corresponding enclosure on the shore nearby, together with a digger and some cones.

"Why would you put a turbine in a lake?" asked Izzy.

"I guess people won't be able to mess with it if it's out in the water," said Monica.

Just up from a free-floating rowing boat, a loose section of the plastic fencing on the island was flapping in the breeze.

"Look," said Monica. "Look there in the gap you can see in the fence. Tell me I'm not imagining things."

Izzy peered. On the uneven concrete surface there was indeed a shoe, ginger and petrol blue. It was upturned, wedge heel pointed at the sky.

"How can it be over there?" said Izzy. "She rowed out in the night?"

Denise Upton came down the path, her cheeks flushed in the cold morning air.

"Cat's not in her room, but Briony reckons her car's still in the car park."

"You don't think she's drowned, do you?" said Monica.

"Bit of a wild conclusion to leap to."

Monica pointed out at the island.

"Hang on," said Denise and pulled a small pair of binoculars from her bag.

"You always carry binoculars?" said Izzy.

"A twitcher is always prepared." She put them to her eyes. "Wait..." she said, and then, a moment later, whispered, "Oh, my..."

She lowered the binoculars and swallowed drily. "We need to call..." she began. "Oh, I don't know who we need to call."

"What is it?" said Izzy, but Denise was already passing her the binoculars.

Izzy put them to her eyes, took a moment to find the island and another to focus a little. She couldn't see what Denise had been so shocked by. Yes, there was Cat's shoe and...

"Oh, my..." she said, echoing Denise's words.

There were five toes poking out of the end of the shoe. The shoe was still on Cat's foot. And the rest of her, as far as Izzy could tell, was buried beneath the concrete.

6

"She did what?!" said Penny.

Izzy gave a tired and miserable shrug. Penny could see the weight of the last few hours falling heavily on her cousin's shoulders. She emerged at once from behind the counter at the Cozy Craft sewing shop, and wrapped Izzy in a huge hug. Izzy fell into it gratefully, almost pushing Penny back.

Izzy began to say something but her face was buried in Penny's woolly cardigan, and all Penny heard was, "Mmm mff-mfff mhmn mff-n-mmm."

"What was that?"

Izzy pulled back, and now there were big tear-smeared rings around her eyes.

"You need a sit down and a restorative drink," said Penny.

She put the 'Closed' sign up on the shop door (the cold January wind rattling through the streets of Framlingham had made most shoppers stay at home anyway) and took

Izzy up to her own rooms on the second floor of the building.

Penny had been living above the shop ever since she agreed to Nanna Lem's request to take over running the place nearly a year ago. The second floor had enough space for a fabric store room, a recently redecorated bathroom and a large front room that served as both bedroom and lounge. There were two comfy chairs by the front window, and Penny made Izzy sit down while she went to the kitchenette to make two large mugs of hot chocolate.

Making hot chocolate and searching for a packet of biscuits gave Penny time to process what Izzy had just told her. One of the hen party guests, Catriona Wallerton, proprietor of the cake shop, was dead, apparently drowned in concrete. It was incredible and shocking.

Izzy had turned on the little fan heater on the floor and put her feet in front of it. It was true that the room was quite cold. There was a wintry draught coming in from somewhere. Monty, the shop's little corgi dog, waddled over and flopped on the floor between the heater and Izzy's feet. Izzy made a soft noise and tucked her feet under the furry hound.

Izzy held the offered hot chocolate in both hands and smiled at its pleasant warmth. It was just after lunch, and Izzy looked like she hadn't slept in days.

"The police only let us go an hour ago," she said. "Local officers came to take initial statements and check our contact details."

"What could have possibly happened?" asked Penny. She wanted to add that she knew some crazy things went on over hen and stag weekends, but drowning in concrete seemed considerably wilder than inflatable sex dolls and handcuffing someone to a lamppost in only their underpants.

"It's just incomprehensible," said Izzy after a slow sip of steaming hot chocolate. "We all went to bed in our little lodges. They're sort of cabins, small but luxurious, but then in the night, I guess…" She stared with tired eyes. "The obvious explanation, crazy though it seems, is that she got up in the night and walked down to the lake. She must have rowed out to the centre island. She could have swum I suppose, but… And then, on the island, she either accidentally or deliberately stepped into the concrete foundations they were pouring for the wind turbine. We could see her footprints on the concrete. Dr Upton had some bird-watching binoculars. And she…"

As if in sympathy, Monty whined and snuggled up against Izzy's ankles.

"That almost sounds like suicide," said Penny.

Izzy began to eat the biscuits on the plate, munching in the manner of someone who needed the energy.

"Or maybe she had just meant to go for a late night walk," said Penny.

"As far as I'm aware, Cat never did anything in life without an audience. Very much the centre of attention. Did you know her in school?"

Penny shook her heads. "Not really. Different year groups." Penny and Izzy had both grown up in Framlingham. Everyone didn't really know everyone else in the small town in the hedgerow-lined farmland of Suffolk, but sometimes it felt like they did. "I've been in the cake shop, obviously."

Izzy blinked, struck by a thought. "I wondered if she'd already made Briony's wedding cake before she died or if they'll have to go somewhere else —" She stopped herself. "That's a small and petty thought, Izzy King."

Penny shook her head. "Something like this could put a dint in anyone's wedding plans. Cat was going to be a bridesmaid, wasn't she?"

"Along with Olivia and Denise Upton. A statuesque bunch of girls."

The mention of statues turned Penny's thoughts tastelessly to Cat in the concrete.

"Had the concrete set?" she asked.

"I think they were having to get someone to come over and dig her out," said Izzy. "Might be days before they fully recover her." Izzy stuffed the last biscuit into her mouth. "Sorry," she said around a mouthful of ginger nut biscuit.

"Not a worry. Let me get some more."

Penny took the plate. Izzy leaned forward and tickled Monty between the ears. The wind whistled through the window and the almost empty marketplace down below.

When Penny returned with some golden crunch cream biscuits a minute later, Izzy was fast asleep in her chair. Penny put the biscuits down and found a warm crocheted blanket to put over her cousin's knees.

7

Penny woke up on Monday morning and edged an arm out of bed to find that it was unusually cold. Her room was heated by an oil filled radiator on a timer, so she assumed that she had woken up early. When she checked the clock she saw it was in fact time to get up. She dashed across to check the radiator, and it was definitely on, but the chill in the flat had overwhelmed it. She knew that it wouldn't go any higher, and rushed through her morning routine at top speed so that she could get herself dressed in something warm. Monty the corgi seemed cosy enough in his basket, but when they went downstairs and outside, he hesitated at the biting wind that whisked the air as Penny cracked the door open. They ventured outside for the briefest of walks, and then Monty decided it was breakfast time.

Penny made sure that the shop itself would be warm

enough for customers, but the lower floors were much less exposed to draughts.

Izzy parked her yarn-covered bicycle outside the front and came in, stamping her feet on the doormat. "It's a cold one today!" she exclaimed.

She looked much better than she had done two days earlier. The shock of Cat's death had mostly worked its way through her system and Izzy was, as best as Penny could tell, back to her usual self.

The door chimed. Aubrey Jones, local decorator and handyman, stepped inside, a heavy paint-spattered toolbox in his hand.

"Morning," said Penny.

"It's a cold one today!" he said. There was a rosy glow to the cheeks on his handsome, easy-going face.

Penny laughed. "You both said the exact same thing."

"Well it *is* cold," he said. "I've been getting the final coat on the exterior paintwork of Sally Butterwick's shop."

Sal Butterwick had inherited the shop at the end of the row from her uncle. He had run it as a record and rock memorabilia shop. It wasn't yet known what kind of shop Sal wanted it to be.

"Have you just come down here to warm up?" asked Penny.

"Maybe pop in and see my favourite seamstresses," he said.

"Seamstresses!" said Izzy in mock outrage.

"And maybe see if I can get a warming cup of tea to put some life back in my fingers," he admitted.

Penny headed upstairs to put the kettle on in the

kitchenette. "Well, my flat is freezing in this weather," she said as she went. "The little radiator just can't seem to hack it when it's both windy and cold."

She made three cups of tea, adding a splash of soya milk for Aubrey. She brought them down on a tray.

"Yours is in the travel mug," she told Aubrey.

"You are an amazing woman," he said.

Izzy, sorting things out behind the till, waggled her eyebrows suggestively at Penny.

"Is your room draught-proofed?" asked Aubrey.

"It most certainly is!" said Izzy. "I made Carruthers the Caterpillar for the bottom of the door, didn't I Penny?"

"You did," Penny agreed. Carruthers was a draught excluder in the shape of a comedy caterpillar. Izzy had given it a hilarious face with huge expressive eyes. What Penny didn't mention was that Carruthers was made from a faux fur fabric that shed annoying little fibres everywhere, and as a result she had reluctantly banished it to the bottom of her wardrobe.

"You shouldn't be cold," said Aubrey with a frown.

"No woman should be cold, should she?" said Izzy, archly.

"I must see if I can do something." He raised the thermos travel mug in thanks. "This is great."

"I think your favourite painter and decorator has plans to keep you warm at night," said Izzy after he'd left. "That sounds as if it could be fun."

Penny rolled her eyes. "I'm not sure what he has in mind, Izzy, but I doubt it's what you're thinking of. Although I don't know what he could do to the room, given this is a listed building."

"The answer is obvious then," said Izzy. "He's offering his snuggling services."

Penny gave her a frank look.

"What?" said Izzy. "Have you already signed up for snuggling services from Oscar Connelly?"

Oscar had gone back to London on the Sunday, bright and early. The two men were very different, both physically and in temperament. Right now, Penny thought that a warming snuggle from either of them would be very much appreciated.

Penny spent much of the morning putting stock out on display. A new delivery of thread had arrived, a box full of colours that made her smile.

Izzy walked over. "Ooh, don't they look like delicious sweeties!" She rummaged in the box and pulled out a lucky dip, which turned out to be a pale amber." Don't you think that the sewing thread companies should name the colours, though?"

"They do name them. This one here is three three nine," said Penny, holding up another reel.

"I guess a number is all you can fit on a tiny reel, but it would be fun if they had outlandish names like the posh house paints do. So instead of nine six eight, this one would be called uncooked gingerbread."

"Mmm, gingerbread!" said Penny. "If the threads all had food-based names, we'd spend all of our time going back and forth for snacks."

"True!"

They looked to the door as it opened. Monica Blowers came in, boots clomping on the polished wooden floor.

"Monica, good to see you!" said Izzy. "What colour would you call this?"

Penny held up the reel of thread. Monica looked at it thoughtfully.

"That's an Arizona Tan, as used on Land Rover 90s from eighty-four to eighty-seven," she decided.

"Arizona Tan, then," said Izzy.

"How are you doing?" asked Penny. "I'm really sorry to hear about what happened at the hen do."

Monica sniffed. "Certainly made for a surprising weekend. I didn't really know Catriona, and she wasn't all that nice to me, but I would never wish that on anyone. Drowned in concrete."

"She wasn't nice to you?" said Penny.

"She called me an ugly duckling."

"Some thoughtless words were said when alcohol had been consumed," said Izzy.

Penny grimaced. "That sounds rather callous. Although it does speak of potential, that you're going to become a beautiful swan."

"I wasn't aware I needed to become anything," said Monica. "But there's a wedding coming up and it would appear that a certain bride and some of her bridesmaids think I can't turn heads in a beautiful dress."

It took Penny a moment to realise that by 'dress', Monica meant something from Cozy Craft.

"Oh, you'd like us to create something for you?"

Monica nodded with slow solemnity. "I'm the groom's

sister. I have to be there, apparently. I need an outfit for this wedding. And I'm thinking, what if I really went for it? Like *really* went for it?"

"You want a unique, head-turning, show-stopping outfit," said Izzy.

"Yes! Something that will make people stop and stare. Can you help me?"

Izzy beamed. "You betcha!"

8

Penny suggested that Monica might want to flick through the pattern catalogues, to see if she might gain any initial inspiration for her outfit. Izzy was jotting notes and ideas on a pad at the counter.

"Any favourite colours or points of inspiration?" she asked Monica.

Monica gave it some thought. "I don't really have a favourite colour. If I'm going to be the swan everyone's on about, maybe white would be good."

"Some people might avoid wearing white to a wedding so that they didn't clash with the bride," Penny observed.

"Isn't that idea a bit outdated?" said Izzy. "It's not as if you're going to wear a wedding dress is it?"

"No, definitely not."

"You want a swan dress." Izzy googled *swan dress* to see what came up. "Huh, there's something here you might want to see."

Monica and Penny both came over.

Izzy pointed to the screen. "In 2001, Bjork went to the Oscars in a swan dress. She caused quite a stir, by the looks of it."

"Bjork?" said Monica.

"Mmmm."

The quirky Icelandic singer was smiling at the camera, wearing a dress that appeared to be an actual swan, its neck lovingly curled around her shoulders. Its body was a froth of cloudy white tulle.

"Blimey," said Monica.

Penny peered closer at the screen. "What is she wearing underneath?"

"I think the dress must be built onto a nude-coloured body stocking," said Izzy. "Like dancewear."

"So it's probably pretty comfy?" said Monica. "One of the reasons I can't abide fancy clothes is always being a bit uncomfortable."

"It would be wearable enough, I think," said Izzy.

"So could you make me something like this?" asked Monica.

"Um. What? Are you joking?" Izzy grinned.

"I'm not joking. I said I wanted a stunning dress that would make people look. This is just the ticket."

Penny looked like she wanted to point out that that it took a certain kind of person — a kooky, slender, elfin woman like Bjork — to carry off a swan dress, but Izzy wasn't going to let anyone's dress-related dreams be dashed.

"Now the idea is in my head," Izzy said before Penny could speak, "I really want to make something like this. I would actually pay you to let me make it for you." Izzy caught Penny's look and cleared her throat. "Although obviously we will prepare a quote because we still have to eat."

"Can it have pockets?" asked Monica.

Izzy looked hard at the image on her phone. "Hm. I'm not sure that Bjork's one has pockets. Where would they go? Maybe there's a place where we could — oh!" She stabbed a finger on the swan's head. "What about in here? We could make the head have a little bit of space inside, maybe?"

"It would be good to be able to carry a phone," said Monica. "If nothing else, I want to capture people's reactions to my outfit."

"A phone? that's quite big. Let me think about it, I'll work something out," said Izzy.

Penny had a troubled look on her face. "Don't you think that something this... ostentatious might draw attention away from the bride on her big day?"

Monica gave this some thought. "Can I be honest?"

"Please," said Izzy.

"I don't know if I wholly approve of this marriage between Ross and Briony."

"Oh." This was certainly not the kind of thing one expected to hear in the final weeks before a wedding.

"Oh, Briony is nice enough I guess, and Ross definitely loves her."

"Well, that's good," said Penny.

"But... have either of you got someone in your lives?"

"Izzy's dating a Polish dog trainer," said Penny.

"Penny has spent a year failing to decide if she should

date a hunky painter and decorator or a super clever fabric salesman from London."

"I have not been failing to decide anything," replied Penny in the voice of a woman who had absolutely failed to pick a boyfriend for nearly a year.

"Well, you know love," said Monica. "It's a two-way street. You've got to both love each other."

"You don't think Briony loves Ross?" asked Izzy.

"She likes him. She might even love the idea of being married to him, but..." She sighed, knowing she was about to speak unkind words. "My brother stands to inherit a big share of Dad's farm one day, and he's already got his own land too. He's well respected in land management circles. He's like a professor of farming. Obviously, he's a great big doofus but he's also quite a catch for a woman who wants financial security for herself."

"You think she's marrying for money," said Penny.

Monica shrugged. "It's not a crime, is it? Point is, if she's marrying Ross Blowers then perhaps she needs to be reminded she's marrying the whole Blowers clan." She thrust her arms up and out to her side. "Measure me! We're doing this thing!"

Penny gave Izzy a look. Izzy composed herself and reached for the tape measure.

9

It was a slow week in the Cozy Craft shop. Cold winds kept potential customers at home, and Izzy had pointed out that the weeks after Christmas and New Year were always a bit quieter while people counted the cost of the holiday season and tried to tighten their belts.

"I might go out and draw some swans," Izzy declared on Wednesday morning. "You know, as research for Monica's dress."

"Walking down to the river?" said Penny. "Maybe Monty and I could join you for a bit of a walk."

At the mention of his name and the word 'walk' Monty's big triangular ears perked up.

"Actually," said Izzy, in a slow, almost guilty voice, "I was thinking of going farther afield."

"Oh?"

"Like the lake at Letheringham Hall."

"The wedding venue?"

"Er, yes."

"The scene of the, um..." Penny didn't want to say 'crime'. She didn't know what the correct word was to describe someone being drowned in concrete.

"I need to get some things straight in my mind," said Izzy.

"You want closure on the terrible incident," said Penny.

"Closure? Yes, I need to put the pieces together in my mind."

"Okay. You cycling out there? A bit far for a walk for me and Monty, I guess."

Monty had been well-trained with the guidance of Izzy's boyfriend, Marcin, but not even the smartest dog could understand complex spoken sentences. And yet Monty responded to this with a whiny grumble and sank back into his bed.

Penny began to wrap a warm scarf around her neck in preparation for going out. The shop door opened and Aubrey entered.

"Ah Penny! I have something for you." He put a carrier bag on the counter.

"What's this?"

"It's a gift. You can take a look, it should be just what you need."

"Gifts from a passing handyman?" said Izzy playfully.

Penny opened the top of the carrier bag and couldn't immediately see what the thing inside was, so she pulled it out.

"Oh."

It was pale pink and rubbery to the touch.

"A hot water bottle," said Izzy.

"A hot water bottle," echoed Penny, not sure what to make of it. She forced a smile onto her face.

"You said you were feeling cold in your flat," said Aubrey.

"I did."

"Now, obviously you know to be careful of burns," he said. "Wrap it in a towel when you use it, or maybe you can make a cover for it, after all, you're in the right place." He smiled and waved a hand at the fabric and sewing machines.

"Thank you," said Penny.

"I need to run but I wanted to make sure you had this." He left the shop with a wave.

Izzy came over to take a closer look.

"You said he was going to offer snuggling services," said Penny.

"It's sort of like snuggling services," replied Izzy, trying to sound upbeat. "It's like a snuggle you can take with you anywhere."

Penny was unconvinced. She hurried to the door. On the road outside, Aubrey was climbing into his van.

"Aubrey, thanks for the gift."

"Not a problem."

She waved her hands at his vehicle. "Are you busy? Is there any chance you could run Izzy and me down to Letheringham Hall."

He looked like he was momentarily torn, but then smiled and gestured. "Of course. Hop in."

10

Izzy circled the lake at Letheringham Hall, trying to get closer to the pair of swans that glided serenely across its surface. She had a bag with some crusts of bread along with her sketchbook and pencils.

Penny and Monty had come down to the lake with her, but Monty's presence was driving the birds to the other side of the lake and Penny had agreed to take him off for a walk in the woods while Izzy sketched.

The lake surface was still, like a polished iron mirror. The birds left barely a ripple as they moved. She felt certain that they were tracking her movements, but deliberately staying thirty feet out, making it difficult to see the detail of their heads, which was what she needed if she was going to sketch them for Monica's outfit. She went to the edge and pulled out a crust. She waved it in the air to catch their attention, then broke off a piece and threw it into the water. One of the swans moved towards the crumb and dipped its long neck to scoop it up. She got another piece ready, the bird watching her movements carefully. Its companion came closer, too. Izzy threw the crumb, landing it a little closer to her own position. Her ploy worked, and the birds came closer still. She kept going, determined to draw them as close to her as possible. She wondered if she was putting all of her effort into luring the birds closer to put off the moment when she would have to apply pencil to paper.

She sighed and pulled out her sketch pad. Izzy's mental visions never seemed to quite match the physical renderings she was capable of. She should capture the curve of the neck and get the shape of the head just right. Pinning the edge of her pad against her chest with gloved hands, she made some tentative strokes on the paper. No, she realised immediately, she'd made it look stocky, like a pigeon. She could do a close up of the head. She worked backwards from its beak and the black mask around its eyes like a cartoon burglar. She paused and gave it a long critical look. She had been so invested in the mask, she had drawn a Zorro swan.

She worked on a series of beaks. Surely she could get the beak sorted out if she focused on capturing the shape and the colour? Her coloured pencils didn't contain an exact match, so she coloured them in with the pale red and added a note that said *Heinz Tomato Soup* as a reminder of the colour she should use.

The swans had eaten the bread and were moving closer now, in a way that was quite menacing.

"Back off, I'll get you some more in a minute!" she said. One of them reared up and flapped its wings at her, taking the aggression up another notch.

"Wow! No wonder I'm the only one out here doing this. Have you scared off all the other wildlife lovers? You know you'd get more snacks if you were nicer to people?"

She broke up the rest of the bread, scattered it on the water, then pulled out her phone to take some snaps.

"Talking to the wildlife?" said Penny, ambling up to her.

"They were starting to get a bit feisty," said Izzy.

"Swans do have a reputation for being simultaneously aloof and aggressive. Are they the ones that can break a person's arm with their wing? Or is that geese?"

"I'm not sure that it's either."

Monty, who had muddy feet and appeared to be having the time of his life, scampered to the lakeside and barked at the swans. The swans, pretending not to care, drifted away.

Penny pointed at the island at the centre of the lake. "Is that where...?"

Izzy nodded.

It was clear there had been plenty of activity on the island recently. The flat block of concrete that was supposed to be the foundation for the wind turbine had been hollowed out. On the lake shore, to one side, the removed sections had been piled up like a modern art installation.

"I don't even know who would have to do a job like that," said Penny in fascinated horror. "The paramedics? The police? They'd have had to let Cat's family know as well." She looked to Izzy. "Do you know if she had any family?"

Izzy frowned. "Not much. The other staff at the cake shop. I think her mum's still alive. She had Cat later in life. In fact, I think she's at Miller's Field like Nanna Lem. Suffers with dementia, if I remember."

"Very sad."

The walked round the lake together.

"How many of you were at the lodges altogether?" Penny asked.

"Um. Seven. Me, Monica, Cat, Briony, her mum Shirley, Doctor Denise Upton and cousin Olivia, who was throwing up that night because Cat had fed her bacon-flavoured cornbread."

"All in separate lodges?"

"All apart from Briony and Shirley, who shared a big one. We all had our own little houses."

They were coming up to the pile of concrete rubble on the bank of the lake, a series of irregular dried objects. To Penny's eye, it looked like they had been soft and clay-like when dug out but had now finally dried out in smooth, sculpted shapes.

Penny saw a pair of shoe imprints in a large section. "A footprint," she said and took a photo of it on her phone.

Izzy nodded. "We thought we could see footprints in the concrete that morning. Cat must have come down here with only one shoe or…" She frowned and then tried to explain the business with the shoe she'd found on the path before breakfast.

"That is odd," Penny agreed.

"What's odd is that no one else remembers seeing it and no one took it."

"Maybe a thieving magpie swooped down and took it…"

"These were chunky wedge heels," said Izzy. "Even a big bird, even a… a hawk would have trouble lifting it."

Penny looked up at the trees, imagining the guest lodges

and the hotel beyond. "So, either Cat left her lodge, lost her shoe, went back for it after you'd gone off for breakfast and then came out here, walked across the concrete and drowned."

"But Monica had already seen her before breakfast." Izzy pointed out at the lake.

"Right. Yes. So Cat left her lodge at some point in the night, dropped her shoe, came down here with only one shoe on, went out onto the concrete and drowned *and then* someone else removed the shoe you saw."

"You're not going to suggest I made the whole shoe thing up? Imagined it?" said Izzy, surprised.

"You are many things, Izzy. You are deeply unconventional at times and constantly powered by an untamed imagination —"

"Thank you."

"— but you're not an idiot and you're not a liar."

"I'm glad you noticed."

Monty danced at their feet, yipping.

"The young master wants a walk," said Izzy. "Shall we go and find some sticks to throw?"

11

Grey clouds lowered over Letheringham Hall as Penny and Izzy walked up the hill. Penny didn't know the history of the place, but it looked like the kind of house a rich industrialist or landowner might have built for themselves two hundred years ago because they were jealous of the castles and palaces that the real aristocracy had. It had many of the fancy ornamentations of a much older building, but couldn't disguise the fact that it was basically an enormous house with proper gutters and indoor plumbing.

Their feet crunched on the gravel as they crossed the driveway at the front of the hall.

"Izzy?"

The shout had come from a woman who had just emerged from a Mercedes Benz. Penny recognised her as Briony Hart, the bride-to-be, which probably made the older woman with her the mother, Shirley.

"Briony!" Izzy replied and hurried over.

The two old school friends fell into a hug.

"How are you holding up?" said Briony. "I can't stop thinking..."

"I know, I know," said Izzy. "Still shocked."

"As if we don't have enough to worry about..." began Shirley primly, and then clearly heard the tactlessness in her own words and shut down the sentence before she could finish it.

"It's all very sad," said Penny.

The two women looked at her. Penny held out her hand to shake.

"Penny Slipper. Izzy's cousin. We run the sewing shop together."

"Ah, the famous Penny," said Briony and shook hands.

"Sacrificed your career in London to help out at your grandma's shop," said Shirley.

Penny wouldn't have described her life choices in quite that way. She hadn't so much sacrificed her job in London as fled from its tattered ruins. But Shirley's version sounded better.

"We've just come down to sort out some things with the events manager," said Briony. "Have you seen the room we're getting married in? You must!"

And so, without much room for argument, Penny and Izzy were escorted inside.

"We're having both the wedding ceremony and the reception in the orangery," Briony explained as they moved through the plushly carpeted reception area and towards the rear of the house. "Ceremony. Chairs cleared aside and then a wedding reception and dance."

"You need to pick a song for your first dance, still," Shirley reminded her.

Briony nodded. "I'd quite like 'Thinking Out Loud' by Ed Sheeran. Mum here prefers 'All of Me' by John Legend."

"What does Ross think?" asked Izzy.

The mother and daughter laughed. "Ross doesn't have much of an opinion on such things. He doesn't have firm opinions on anything."

"Pigs in blankets on the reception menu," said Shirley.

"True," said Briony. "He was very firm on that."

"Our Briony is a lovely dancer."

"You used to be big into your dancing as a teenager," said Izzy and Penny had vague recollections of slender goody-two-shoes Briony Hart being called up on stage in school to be presented with dancing trophies or certificates or somesuch.

"Well, we all know why you stopped doing that," said Shirley with some bitterness.

"A childhood hobby," said Briony. "I can't be a successful dancer *and* run a soap-making company, can I?"

Penny would have expected an orangery to be a relatively small space, a simple greenhouse attached to the back of the property, but clearly the architect had been consumed by a grander inspiration. The orangery would have been large enough to host a small tennis tournament, although the high windows and glass domed ceiling might have lost a pane or two if it had. The place was light and cheery, although Penny noticed it was currently quite cold.

"This is beautiful," she said.

"Isn't it?" said Shirley. "Cost enough, too."

"I can assure you we are giving you our absolute best rate," said a suited man, entering the room.

"At the mention of money, the hotel manager appears," said Shirley.

"Events manager," said the man. His long face lent him an air of seriousness that was broken by his frequent smiles.

"James, you remember Izzy? This is her cousin, Penny."

James shook Penny's hand. "I believe we went to the same school. James Coombes."

"Oh, I'm sorry. I don't recall," said Penny.

"It's okay," he smiled. "I was one of those forgettable people, always in the background." He whipped out a clipboard from under his arm. "I think we have all the plans in order. I was sent through the floral layout from Bellforth's."

As Briony looked over the plans, Izzy said to Penny. "You know cousin Olivia's boyfriend?"

"Gavin? The one who never comes to family events?"

"He's doing the flowers," said Izzy. "What with Cat doing the cake and James getting them the venue, I think Briony and Shirley have roped in every old friend and personal connection they could find to organise this wedding."

She turned to Shirley. "The wedding cake...?"

Shirley understood immediately. "I was trying to find the right time to pop into the bakery and ask. How does one put it delicately? Yes, I know your owner and chief cake-maker is dead, but are you still going to give us a wedding cake? There's no book on etiquette that covers that one."

"And she was going to be a bridesmaid too, wasn't she?" said Penny.

Shirley pulled a funny face. "Well, as per usual, Cat bullied and wheedled her way into that role. Quite the manipulator, she was. Yes, I know she's dead and that is honestly very sad indeed, but she was never a positive influence on Briony's life."

"Really?"

"In life, we reap what we sow, and I don't think Cat sowed much goodness in hers. In fact, I'm surprised that Briony let Cat and Gavin both be so involved with the wedding plans, you know."

Penny did want to ask what that meant, but Briony and James had found a point of discussion in the planning and a clipboard was being thrust in front of Shirley.

"James was saying he needs to formalise the seating plans," said Briony.

"Or at least the numbers," he said. "I had a list of names, but I know you were adding to it. I've had some extras sent over by the groom."

"The groom?" said Shirley. "I wasn't aware he had any more friends left to invite."

"The Blowers are somewhat under-represented, though," said James.

"You know you're on here?" said Briony and it took Penny a moment or two to realise that Briony was talking to her.

"Me?" said Penny.

"Penny Slipper plus one," said James. "I was told quite explicitly to underline the 'plus one' part."

Penny was confused for a moment, and then she

understood. She could sense Monica's hand in this. When they'd been talking about dresses, Izzy had made much of Penny's supposed indecision regarding her supposed romantic interest in Aubrey and Oscar. And Monica had no doubt thought it hilarious to tell her brother to stick Penny on the invite list and see which man she brought with her.

Penny didn't know whether to laugh or to scowl in fury. Izzy's eyes were dancing with mirth.

"An invite for me?" said Penny neutrally. "How lovely!"

12

Wrapped up in a warm knitted cardigan and with a morning cup of coffee steaming on the counter, Penny pored over Izzy's sketches for the swan dress. It was clear that Izzy had put a lot of thought into this, showing the design from different directions, with notes about how they would go about making Monica's version of the iconic dress.

"So the head and neck of the swan will be made separately and then joined on?"

"Yes, that part is going to be more like a stuffed toy than a garment. We might need some wire inside to get it to curve around in the way we want it to."

"You've written some notes on the fabric choice. White plush, yeah?"

"I think so. We find some plush or polar fleece or maybe even faux fur that we can trim back. Whatever looks most like a swan. The detail on the face will be small pieces of felt or something similar."

Penny tapped a message to Oscar, asking what textured fabric he might have available if she wished to create a swan. She smiled as she did so, knowing how much he enjoyed the bizarre questions they often sent his way.

"Then there's the bottom part of the, er, swan. I see question marks here, what's that all about?" asked Penny.

"Well, we might have to play it by ear a little. We set all of these tulle strips onto the base, right?"

"Right."

"And we probably keep going until it looks floofy enough."

"Maximum floof."

"So the thing that I don't know," said Izzy, "is how heavy that's going to be. If it weighs a lot then we need to build in some way of supporting it. We can't have it sagging in on itself."

"Good point. How do we support it?"

"With a foundation underneath, which will probably have to include boning."

"A foundation! That sounds a bit old-fashioned and uncomfortable," said Penny.

"No, it sounds like couture," replied Izzy, "and if we do it correctly, it will pass Monica's comfort requirements."

For much of that afternoon, Penny puzzled over the best fabric to use for the bodysuit.

"I've got some fabric samples for the leotard," she called to Izzy.

"Ooh nice, let's see."

Penny laid them out on the counter. She had already decided which she favoured and had sent pictures of them to Oscar, but she wanted to see whether Izzy would agree with her choices.

"They're all a good match to Monica's skin colour," said Izzy. "Do they all have stretch?"

She went down the line, pulling them in both directions to test the stretch properties of the fabric. She grunted, satisfied that they would all perform as needed.

"So the main question you're considering is how dense it should look on the skin, and do we want a fabric with sparkles already on it?"

Penny nodded. Some of the fabrics were plain nude, and others were shot through with glittery silver or gold threads.

Izzy pulled up a sleeve and placed each sample against her arm, smoothing them into place so that she could see how it looked on skin. "I can't imagine Monica enjoying the all-over glitter look."

"Yeah, I agree. Fine if you're a figure skater, but this shouldn't distract the eye from the swan dress," agreed Penny.

"Well put," said Izzy. "On that same basis, we want the lightest possible touch, so I reckon this very fine one here is my favourite." She pointed at one of the samples.

"Perfect, that was my choice too," beamed Penny. "I'll get it ordered so I can crack on and make the leotard. I can add some sparkly motifs with rhinestones after construction. Maybe Monica has some favourite shapes we could put on."

Penny saw Izzy's face and realised what she was thinking.

"No. No, we're definitely not having a rhinestone Land Rover on here. Definitely not."

All in all, it turned out to be a productive day. The January weather outside was horribly unwelcoming and Monty was content for his walks to consist of swift turns around Market Hill and a brief trot up through the church yard to the castle grounds. That aside, it was a day for staying in and keeping warm.

13

At the end of the day, with all the designs and experimental fabrics tidied neatly away, Izzy cycled home. It would be Rogers and Hammerstein night at the King residence, a hearty meal followed by Izzy's mum and dad banging out old show tunes on keyboard and guitar and Izzy singing along with gusto. Penny had experienced it before and, while it was an evening of familial love and fun, there was only so much room for twentieth century musicals in her life.

Penny decided her own evening would be spent snuggled up with a good book and her favourite dog. She heated up a sponge pudding and custard for her evening dessert and boiled the kettle to fill her new hot water bottle. Part of her had considered rejecting Aubrey's gift because it was such a... well, it was an old lady gift, a stay-at-home-and-do-nothing gift. And, yes, she was staying home and doing nothing but, still, the sentiment behind it grated. And yet, wrapped in a crocheted throw and tucked up in her armchair by the window, it was pleasantly warm and took the chill off her draughty room.

She sent a text to Aubrey to give additional thanks for the present. He replied immediately with humble words and a cheery emoji.

Her dessert finished, Penny looked out of the window. Out in the middle of the market place, by the old cross, she could see Old McGillicuddy and Timmy sitting in their usual spot. The elderly man and his equally elderly dog seemed to keep a vigil there every morning and every evening. Penny had been assured that they had a home to go to, otherwise she'd have been rushing out to offer them hot drinks on a regular basis. Come rain or shine, the two of them kept up their habits.

The good book she had intended to curl up with was one that Annalise at the library had insisted she would like. However, Penny soon found herself confused by the excessive number of characters, and felt like giving up. With little hesitation, she put it aside, and picked up the weighty scrap book Oscar had brought back with him from his New York trip.

She flicked through the heavy pages of polaroid photos and various receipts, samples and souvenirs. She'd sent Oscar a number of messages during the day but he'd not replied to many. She sent him another, asking what fabrics might best be used to make the swan's head on Monica's dress.

Within a minute, her phone was ringing.

"Hello!" she said.

There was considerable noise and chatter in the background.

"Hi," said Oscar. "Hang on."

There were rumbles and clicks, and then the noise was quieter.

"Sorry," he said. "At a friend's house party in Hammersmith."

"Oh, I didn't mean to pull you away," said Penny.

"Lord, no. Very dull affair. I'm here more out of duty than desire. A friend wanted to talk to me about a job. But now I've ensconced myself in what appears to be... hmm, I'm going to go with 'yoga room'. Or maybe it's a home office, but without chairs. How are things?"

"Things are, er, fine," said Penny. The noise and bustle and excitement of Oscar's evening suddenly made Penny feel that hers was dull and deathly quiet. "Busy day trying to work out how to construct a Bjork swan dress."

"Sounds genuinely exciting."

"Says the man at the heart of the London fashion scene."

He laughed. "It probably sounds patronising, but I think you're lucky that you get to work on projects unchained from the demands of fashion."

"Ah, saying I'm unfashionable, are you?" she asked, playfully.

"Not at all. Anyway, unfashionable is to be living in the past. Fashion is to be living in the present, doing what everyone else is doing."

"Right. So Izzy and I live in some sort of couture far future, do we?"

"More a parallel dimension," he suggested with an audible smirk. "What's the dress for?"

"It's for a woman attending a wedding at the end of the month."

"But not the bride? So, she's wearing a white swan to someone else's wedding."

"I know! Is that crazy?"

"Bold," said Oscar, "but I approve. Weddings are the worst!"

"You don't like them?"

"Oh, I like them," he said. "I am a big fan of declarations of love and lifelong commitments. What I don't understand is the slavish adherence to the fashions of bygone eras. The white wedding dress? That's Queen Victoria's fault and she's long gone. And as for men in their morning suits... ugh, is there any other modern cultural scenario that requires men to wear nineteenth century frock coats?"

Penny was amused. "You have strong opinions on the matter."

"I abhor people doing things just because that's the way they've always been done. It stinks of a lack of imagination."

"I'll remind you to never say that to the happy couple if I ever invite you to a wedding," she said, then caught herself.

Until that moment, she'd managed to push Monica's engineered wedding invite from her mind, and here was her subconscious one step away from asking Oscar to be her plus-one on the twenty-seventh. Oh, he would be a fine plus-one, but she had another perhaps equally deserving one on the doorstep, in the shape of Aubrey Jones. In her confusion and embarrassment, she faltered.

"I, er, was looking through your New York scrapbook," she said.

"Glad you like it," he said. "That's why I've ended up at this party."

"Oh?"

"Turns out a friend of a friend has connections with a much admired fabric supplier in the Garment District and, well, said friend of a friend has it in their head that I should be working there."

"Someone's offered you a job in New York?" Penny's words came out in shocked surprise.

"No, not at all," Oscar laughed. "There is no job, only the idle talk of people who love flashing around their industry connections. Nonetheless, it's fun to discuss. Anyway, how could I help you with crazy dress commissions if I'm in completely the wrong time zone?"

"Well, exactly!" said Penny, hoping she hadn't given the impression she was chiding him for entertaining the 'selfish' notion of moving away.

"Linen," said Oscar.

"Pardon?"

"Simple linen is the way I would go with your swan's head."

"Really? Because Izzy had some really interesting thoughts about felt and faux fur."

"Maybe," he said. "And I do think you should trust your instincts on that. But, me, I would consider the general impression you want to give. Dressmaking isn't always about the tiny details, the little rhinestone flourishes or crazy cut-out shapes. This dress, the original, was perhaps inspired by

Swan Lake."

"I suppose so."

"If we think about the ballet dancers and the backdrops, simple fabrics and simple painted designs could convey whole magical worlds."

"Perhaps…"

"Sometimes, we get hung up on the individual details, but if we just step back and view the thing with some perspective, it's the overall impression that counts."

"That's very interesting."

In the pause that followed, Penny could hear muffled music and laughter.

"Of course," said Oscar. "Izzy is going to ignore such advice and construct something baroque and wildly complicated, isn't she?"

"Of course, she is," Penny agreed.

"And so she should. Look, I best be getting back to this thing…"

"Right, right. You should. I'm sorry. I didn't mean to waylay you. Besides, my hot water bottle has gone cold."

"Hot water bottle?" he repeated, and there was amusement in his voice.

"Oh, don't," she said. "I know. I'm an old spinster tucked up and ready for bed."

"Huh. Given a choice between here and there, I know where I'd rather be," he said.

Penny felt something flip inside her. She never considered herself to be a girly romantic, but she had no control over her body's response to such remarks.

"What are you doing on Saturday the twenty-seventh?" she said without thinking about it.

"Er, nothing. Why?"

"No reason. Just asking. Good to know."

"Um, okay. Anyway, gotta go."

"Of course. Go. Go. Have fun."

She ended the call and sat there, staring at nothing. She could still sense that feeling circling in her chest. Monty the dog, laid out by her feet, looked up at her. There was a tone of accusation in his eyes.

"What?" she demanded and then got up to refill her hot water bottle.

14

On Thursday afternoon, Izzy walked across the market place, cut through one of the archways and courtyards that linked it to the roads behind, and crossed over to the entrance of Millers Field sheltered accommodation. Nanna Lem had an apartment there, a perfectly snug if modern flat where she could indulge her retirement hobbies and be within easy reach of her many friends.

Nanna Lem wasn't in her apartment today but in the centre's community room, which was generally set out with dozens of comfy armchairs and served as a huge living room with a kitchen on the side. Nanna Lem sat in corner knitting what appeared to be an endless scarf.

Izzy put the cardboard box she had brought with her down on the table in front of Nanna Lem.

"Ooh, brought me treats?" asked the frizzy-haired woman.

"Biscuits. Might go nice with a cup of tea."

"That they shall." Nanna Lem raised her hand and clicked her fingers. "Glenmore. A cup of tea for me and my granddaughter?"

The older black man by the kitchenette serving hatch nodded in understanding. Glenmore Wilson was a one-armed former military man, the editor in chief of the local amateur newspaper and, as best as Izzy could work out, Nanna Lem's boyfriend or whatever it was eighty-year-olds called their romantic partners. He was also, but only in an amateur sense, Izzy's boss, in that he was editor-in-chief of the Frambeat Gazette, to which Izzy herself was a regular and notable, if somewhat erratic, contributor as well as being an indispensable member of the editorial team.

"You can't order him about, Nanna," Izzy whispered. "If nothing else, you've asked him for two teas and he's only got one hand."

"He can use a tray, can't he?" said Nanna Lem simply. "Now, how is my old shop?"

"The old shop is fine," said Izzy. "Penny is finding it a bit cold and draughty."

"Put another scuttle of coal on the fire." Nanna Lem put her hands out to the electric heater by her side. "I come down here to get warm on someone else's dime."

"And all that wool is there for the same purpose," suggested Izzy, looking at the scarf and balls of wool gathered on Nanna Lem's lap.

"It's just a scarf. Not for anyone in particular. Keeping my fingers busy, for the most part. I had thought I might have a go at knitting the world's longest scarf but that's something like three miles long and I don't have time for that. Literally."

"We could use it for some yarn bombing."

"What? Wrap it around a lamppost? Since when did lampposts need keeping warm?"

Izzy was about to explain that yarnbombing was much more about adding vibrant colour to the world (and occasionally making a political point) but then she saw the cheeky glint in Nanna Lem's eye.

"And what have you been up to?" Nanna Lem asked.

Izzy was happy to launch into an explanation of the swan dress that Monica Blowers had commissioned for her brother's wedding to Briony Hart.

"Oh, a unique challenge," Nanna Lem agreed. "Ah, then I think you should take a look over there."

Izzy looked. There was an older chair with massive rip in its main cushion.

"Doesn't that colour remind you of a swan's bill?" asked Nanna Lem.

She was right. The orange vinyl cover was the exact colour of tomato soup or, indeed, a swan's beak.

"It's going away to be reupholstered next Monday," continued Nanna Lem. "No one would mind if you took some."

Izzy had a box-cutter knife in her pocket. With encouraging nods from her grandmother, she went over to the chair, and with four deft strokes, removed a large square of orangey vinyl fabric.

"If you're finished with butchering the furniture?" said Glenmore Wilson, standing directly behind her.

Izzy stood up guiltily. "Nanna Lem said it would be okay."

Glenmore gave Izzy a steely look that suggested it was neither his nor Nanna Lem's position to say whether it was okay or not. Izzy imagined that Glenmore had perfected a steely gaze in his military career and now, as an older man, it had marinated like the last pickled onion in the jar, to become something powerfully penetrating.

"Your tea is on the table," he said and went off back to the kitchen. The unnervingly tart pickled onion glare seemed to hang in the air for a moment even after he had departed. Izzy hurried back to Nanna Lem and folded her stolen vinyl to take away with her.

"Open the biscuits, then," Nanna Lem instructed.

Izzy opened the box. "These are from Wallerton's cake shop. You heard about Catriona Wallerton dying?"

"Strange, sad business." Nanna Lem pulled the box towards herself. The biscuits within were in the shape of cats with iced whiskers.

"The other staff decided to bake a special biscuit in her memory. The money they raise is going to rescue cats."

"Did Cat support the rescue cats, then?"

Izzy shrugged. "No idea. I got the impression that they're just running with the cat thing on account of her name."

Nanna Lem grunted, took one of the biscuits out and nibbled the corner. "You know Irene Wallerton, Cat's mum, is a resident here."

"I think I'd heard that."

"Vascular dementia. Perfectly competent with the little stuff but doesn't really know if she's coming or going. She paid the money to get Cat's shop up and running."

"Oh, I didn't know that."

"Not sure she knew about it either," said Nanna Lem darkly.

Izzy frowned.

"Oh, something dodgy going on there. Irene's doctor was asking questions. Questions about power of attorney and wotnot. It's no coincidence that Cat couldn't afford to set up that shop until she had her mother moved in here, and then, suddenly..." Nanna Lem trailed off, the implication clear. She put down her biscuit, one cat ear nibbled off, and pointed a crooked finger across the way. "That's her."

Four people, two men and two women, sat at a table, playing cards. They were focussed on it with business-like seriousness.

"Does she know Cat is dead?" said Izzy.

"She's got dementia. Doesn't mean she's gone completely doo-lally," said Nanna Lem, and then softened. "Someone told her, yes, and she was distraught beyond reason. Who wouldn't be? Her only daughter had died. But then the next day..." She sighed. "She was back to normal. If you were to ask her about Cat, she would remember and the grief would kick in again immediately. But if you didn't ask her, she would probably get through the whole day without thinking about it."

"That is tragic."

"Is it?" asked Nanna Lem. "Honestly, I don't know. Old age is a tricksy and cruel bugger, Izzy. At least Irene is well loved here."

In the corner, one of the women put down a card triumphantly and there was mild mannered cursing from the others, together with some laughter. The well-built man putting out decorative flowers in the corner turned round and offered some words of congratulations that Izzy couldn't hear from this distance.

"That's Gavin, our Olivia's boyfriend," said Nanna Lem. "Owns the florists in town. Millers Field pay him to put in some cheering blooms every few weeks."

"I didn't realise Olivia had bagged herself a hunk," said Izzy.

"Gentle giant. Wouldn't say boo to a goose. Notice how he never comes to any family events?"

"I have," said Izzy. "He's doing the flowers for Briony Hart's wedding."

"That's still going ahead, even though one of the bridesmaids has just died?"

"Oh, with Briony and her mum at the controls, this wedding is like a steam roller. Nothing's going to stop it."

15

Izzy returned to Cozy Craft in time to help Penny tidy things away and shut up the shop. She wasn't hanging around, as she had a date with Marcin Nowak.

"Is he taking you somewhere nice?" Penny asked as Izzy finished washing up the cups.

"We're not going anywhere," said Izzy. "I'm just going over to his place."

"But I thought you said it was a date?" Penny said.

Izzy smiled. It sometimes felt that she and Penny expected very different things from any given situation.

"It is a date," Izzy insisted. "We will spend the evening together. There will be some chatting, some getting to know each other better, a fun activity. That is the definition of a date, isn't it?"

Penny gave an exasperated shrug, apparently not understanding. As Penny put on the kettle to fill her hot water bottle, Izzy gave a farewell head scratch to Monty and left for the evening. She headed over to Marcin's place, which was slightly outside of the town, just past the Station pub on Station Road.

Izzy buzzed at Marcin's outer gate and went through into the yard of what she guessed had previously been farm buildings, but now served as Marcin's dog training centre.

"Welcome welcome!" said Marcin, standing at the doorway to the house. Marcin had a face that seemed just delighted to meet everyone, whether they had two legs or four, and Izzy was both excited and a little afraid that she had already fallen in love with it.

He placed a kiss on her cheek. "I have prepared some snacks for later."

"That explains the apron," said Izzy.

"It's a very practical thing," said Marcin. "It was on a hook inside the pantry when I moved in. It keeps my clothes clean, so why wouldn't I wear it?"

"It's quite old," noted Izzy, picking up the edge. "A lovely fun design from the fifties or sixties." It featured a flower print in primary colours, and was finished with red binding around the edges. Izzy had not imagined that Marcin could possibly look any cuter, but somehow this apron did the trick.

"Let me show you inside," said Marcin. He led the way through a huge farmhouse kitchen with hidden treats cooling on racks under tea towels. They went into a lounge with oak beams stretched across the ceiling, but the decor was surprisingly modern. There was a huge television and a large corner sofa. There was a bookcase in the corner and Izzy immediately realised she was desperate to check out the titles, but that could come later. She shrugged off her coat. "This is such a gorgeous room. Are we stopping in here?"

Marcin took her coat. "We can, although we can spread out if we need to. Let me show you what we have. He crossed over to the television cabinet. "I have thirty DVDs for you to inspect. All Jane Austen adaptations. We could pick a decade and stick with that, or we could, for instance, look at all of the Pride and Prejudice adaptations in chronological order? You choose." He walked over to a drop-leaf side table. "Here we have a pile of blankets, sheets and quilts. I think you know what to do with these."

"I certainly do!" said Izzy. "Mind if I rearrange the furniture?"

"Not at all," said Marcin. "You might find extra inspiration in the dining room through there."

Izzy poked her head through the door he had indicated and clapped her hands in glee. "Perfect! This is going to be such a great evening."

16

"You had a Jane Austen movie marathon?" said Penny the next morning.

"We did," replied Izzy. "Marcin is a big period drama fan. His grandma loved lavish period films."

"This is the grandma who was a resistance fighter in the Second World War?"

"No, that was great grandma. His grandma was a car fitter in Gdansk. She used to buy black market videos of period dramas back when Poland was still a Soviet state. Tiny Marcin was raised on them."

"And that constitutes a normal date?" said Penny. "Back-to-back Sense and Sensibility and Pride and Prejudice and... and... the other one?"

"We had a lovely time," said Izzy.

The door chimed as it opened. Aubrey Jones stepped in with a cheery "Good morning" for the pair of them.

"Morning," said Izzy.

"What do you think about a back-to-back Jane Austen movie marathon for a date?" asked Penny.

Aubrey looked momentarily non-plussed.

"Um, when were you thinking? I'm kind of busy most evenings this week."

"No," said Penny, suddenly panicked. "I mean hypothetically. Would it constitute a good date?"

"Oh, I see. Um. Is there something nice to drink and somewhere to cosy down?" asked Aubrey.

"There was," said Izzy. "Hot cups of krupnik."

"Krupnik?"

"It's sort of like a super-mead, a medicinal liqueur."

"Sounds delicious," said Aubrey.

"I'm just saying a date should be a bit more... active," said Penny.

"I'll be sure to mention that to Marcin in my formal feedback," said Izzy.

Aubrey smirked. "So, Penny. Have you managed to road test the hot water bottle yet?"

Penny wasn't sure how to answer. It had been really thoughtful of Aubrey to try to help her stay warm this winter. And yet a hot water bottle was a really odd choice of gift. *And yet* it had really kept her warm and cosy in the evening. And yet, she didn't want to encourage Aubrey too much in the personal gift buying stakes, since she'd been one breath away from inviting Oscar to the wedding the other night and it really wasn't fair to string along either of the two men in her life.

"I have," she said. "We took a rather chilly walk around the lake at Letheringham Hall on Wednesday after you dropped us there, and I found myself very much in need of something to warm my tootsies in the evening."

She mentally rolled her eyes at herself at the mention of *tootsies*. Could she not talk normally to people?

"Letheringham Hall?" said Aubrey. "Wasn't that where the baker woman…?"

"It was," said Izzy. "I needed to sketch some swans for a dress we're making, but I suppose I also wanted to get some things straight in my mind."

"A nasty business."

"It makes no sense," said Izzy. "I don't understand why Cat rowed out there and then tried to walk across the concrete."

"Well, you wouldn't have been able to walk across it at all, really," said Aubrey.

"No, she did," said Penny. "I took a photo of her footprints."

"No. You can't both walk on concrete and drown in it. I… show me."

"What?"

"Show me the picture. Please."

Penny dug out her phone and showed him the image she'd taken of the lump of concrete by the lake side.

"You took this on Wednesday," he said. "It's completely dry."

"It was," said Penny.

"But Cat Wallerton drowned in the concrete on Sunday?"

"Well, Saturday night, Sunday morning."

"I'm sorry to have to ask, but her body... was it like, totally submerged? She wasn't just face down?"

"Everything submerged but her foot," said Izzy.

"No. This does not make sense."

"Doesn't it?" asked Penny. "Why not?"

He used his fingers to enlarge the picture, zooming in on the digger in the background. "Skeltons? Are they the builders doing the work out there?"

"I suppose," said Izzy.

"Have you got room in your back yard for a little experiment?" asked Aubrey.

Penny said, "What experiment?" at the same time as Izzy said, "Of course."

"Excellent," said Aubrey and dashed out with such speed that Monty barked at him in startlement.

"I don't think I understood quite what happened there," said Penny.

"I think the key element is that Aubrey thinks watching a Jane Austen movie marathon from the comfort of your own blanket fort is a high quality date."

Penny shook her head in disbelief. "A blanket fort? You never mentioned that!"

Izzy shrugged. "You were already complaining about the Jane Austen marathon. I didn't want to overload you."

"Blanket forts don't exist in the adult world, Izzy, they are indulgences for children, mainly because children don't have to do the laundry."

"Isn't that the exact point, though?" said Izzy. "Being an

adult should mean that you can invest your time and energy into doing things that make you happy, even if it means doing some extra laundry. We should all indulge ourselves once in a while the same way we indulge children. It's good for us."

17

In the afternoon, Izzy refined and enlarged some swan head sketches while Penny served customers. Izzy had found a set of placemats in the charity shop that featured swans gliding serenely on a lake, so she was able to use those as an extra reference. She erected them like a fence around her work area on the counter.

She wanted to be sure that she could create a pattern for the three dimensional shape of the swan's head. If she had a friendly swan that would let her wrap paper around it, the whole thing would be much simpler, but she'd seen how cooperative swans could be. She needed to figure this out on paper.

Izzy suspected that there was a mathematical way to deducing the pattern shape, but she favoured the experimental approach. She had raided the paper recycling and marked out a series of shapes using a thick felt tip. Making a simple V shape worked for the sort of beak that a baby sparrow might have, but the shaping was more subtle on a swan. Izzy cut them out, formed them into what she hoped might be a beak shape, and then used the results to refine her next attempt.

After a while, she had the pattern pieces for the beak and it was time to move onto the head. By the time Penny peered over her shoulder to see what she was doing, she was confident she could construct a fabric swan's head.

"Check this out." Izzy formed her paper patterns into the beak and the head and held them up to demonstrate. "I'll add a seam allowance, and I'll be away."

"That looks really good!" said Penny. "I'll get to work on the bodysuit in a short while."

They had decided that as the outfit was two completely separate garments, they might as well split the work between them. Penny would make the bodysuit, which would be based on a leotard pattern and sewn from nude-coloured stretch fabric, while Izzy would make the swan head and dress. Penny had promised to lend a hand when it came to gathering tulle for the swan body because that promised to be a large part of the effort needed.

Izzy was on a roll with her new pattern pieces, so she decided to get started on the swan head. She unrolled the orange vinyl that she had recovered from Millers Field. What an eye Nanna Lem had! Izzy considered herself to be something of a dab hand at recycling things, but of course, Nanna Lem had been doing it for years. Izzy reckoned there was more than enough vinyl for her to have two attempts at the swan head, which gave her the confidence to cut into it. The vinyl was fairly thick, so she used the treadle sewing machine to sew the seams. When she trimmed it and turned it through, she grinned and moved on to the rest of the head. She'd decided to construct the whole thing in the white polar fleece and then to add the black mask afterwards.

What about the eyes, though? Izzy went back to consult her reference pictures, gazing across at all the swans on her place mat fence. The eyes were very small and very black. Who knew what went on behind those tiny eyes, apart from malicious thoughts of intimidating passers-by for their bread?

"Hey, Penny!" she called.

"Yeah?"

"You know how Monica wants to capture people's reactions to her swan dress?" Izzy was forming the thought even as she was saying it out loud. "What if we made the swan's head so that the eye was a camera?"

There was a long, silent pause. Izzy raised her head from her swan barricade to see what Penny's face looked like. Was she rolling her eyes at another hare-brained scheme, or had she knocked herself out as she jumped up to congratulate Izzy on a brilliant idea?

She was somewhere in the middle, nodding thoughtfully.

"Let me tell you where my thoughts are on this," said Penny. "My first instinct was that it's crazy and wrong. Then I put myself in our customer's shoes and I can see how it solves a problem for Monica. Then I wondered if it's even legal to do that." She looked up at Izzy. "By the way, it's an awesome idea and I can already see that you're itching to try it."

"We ran a story in the Frambeat Gazette about

surveillance. Britain apparently has a higher coverage of CCTV cameras than anywhere else in the world."

"Uh huh. How will it even work?" asked Penny.

Izzy picked up one of her sketches. "See here, I make an eyelet hole where the swan's eye is, and that's where the camera sits in a little internal pocket. Either we see if Monica's smartphone will fit in there, or we find some other sort of camera that is smaller."

"From a spy shop?"

"Pretty sure you can just get them from big shops or online," said Izzy, waving her hands vaguely. She remembered young Tariq at the Frambeat Gazette getting hot under the collar about the erosion of civil liberties.

"Let's ask Monica what she thinks," said Penny.

A few minutes later, Izzy punched the air. "Yes! Monica says that I am a fairy godmother of inventive goodness, and have I ever thought of designing Land Rover accessories. Huh."

"Maybe that's something to look at another day," said Penny.

"Yes, you're right. I will crack on with my spycam swan for now."

Aubrey strode into the shop.

"Experiment time," he declared.

"Pardon?" said Penny.

"I want to show you something. Come."

He waved them to follow him out of the shop. Penny, mildly irritated at being distracted from her work but overwhelmingly curious, put her things aside and stepped outside.

"You might want your coat," Aubrey said.

Together the three of them (Monty had no intention of stepping outside again today) went out of the shop and up the small alley at the side that ultimately led to the churchyard, but then cut down the narrow passageway that passed along the back of the shops. Aubrey opened the gate to the little backyard of Cozy Craft. It was a space they never used at all and Penny was now surprised to see that it held four plastic tubs, each containing twelve inches of freshly poured concrete.

"I know this looks extravagant," said Aubrey.

"It looks a bit mad," said Penny.

"And we approve of a little madness in life," added Izzy.

Aubrey gestured to the tubs. "What do you know about concrete?"

Izzy shrugged. "It's grey and sticky and you can build things from it."

"It's caustic," said Penny. "It burns if you get cement powder on you."

"It does. It's a powerful alkali and can burn skin. Also, when it dries it causes an exothermic reaction. Drying concrete is surprisingly warm. And, at certain consistencies, it's a non-Newtonian liquid."

"What's that?" asked Penny.

"Oh, like custard," said Izzy.

Penny was about to ask what nonsense she was on about but Aubrey was nodding. "Just like custard."

"Excuse me?" said Penny.

Aubrey crouched. "I can't guarantee this will work." He punched the surface of one of the tubs hard and his hand was halted only a centimetre or two into the liquid. He then withdrew his hand, extending his fingers and pushing them in gently. They sank with ease.

"It's like quicksand. You can, theoretically, run over it quickly, but also sink into it if you're standing still. But only when it's like this." He washed his hand off with a watering can. "I spoke to my mate who works at Skeltons builders. They poured the concrete on Friday and it was this brand of cement they used. I had to check because they have different drying times."

"This is all very fascinating —" said Penny, and then caught a look from Izzy. "No, it really is fascinating, but I feel you're trying to make a point, Aubrey, and I don't know what it is."

He picked up a brick from beside the fence, placed it on top of one of the tubs of cement, and let it sink. It disappeared within a second and the grey gloop flowed over to fill the space.

"If Cat had fallen into the mix on Thursday night or Friday morning, she would have sunk like that, gone completely. Concrete tends to take a day or two to mostly set. It's longer in cold weather. The size and depth of the concrete is also a factor. We don't really have room to replicate what was happening at Letheringham Hall but the principle is the same."

Penny was beginning to understand. "You're saying that by Friday night it would have dried too much for her to sink in like that."

Aubrey gave a cagey shrug. "However gloopy the liquid, human beings often float. And I would argue that if the concrete was dense enough for her to leave footprints then it was also too dense for her to sink in." He consulted his watch. "The concrete for the wind turbine at Letheringham Hall was poured a week ago." He gestured to the pile of bricks by the fence. "May I suggest placing a brick on the concrete every ten or twelve hours, see what happens to each, and then you tell me in a couple of days if it was possible for Cat Wallerton to have sunk unaided into this stuff."

Unaided, thought Penny. If Aubrey's hypothesis was correct, the alternative was that Cat had been *aided* into the drying cement. Pushed down.

"Are we saying she was murdered?" she said.

"I don't know," replied Aubrey. He stood up. "This was fun. I mean the experiment, not the thought of murder, obviously."

"Obviously," said Izzy.

"You two always seem to be involved in the most intriguing things. I'm just happy to be a part of it."

There was an honest smile on his face. Aubrey might have been a decorator and handyman, but Penny was always impressed, even jealous, perhaps, of the simple joy he took in all things. It was one of the things that made him an easy man to like.

"What are you doing on Saturday the twenty-seventh?" Penny asked.

He blinked. "Don't know. Nothing special. Why?"

"Nothing. Just asking."

He brushed the last of the water and crumbs of cement from his hands. "I suppose I ought to actually get back to work. Stuart Dinktrout has asked me to repaint his prized pig's pen before Monday."

"Prize piggy palace," added Izzy, who had seen the garden centre owner's pampered pig's home before.

"Tell me about it," Aubrey smiled. He threw them a casual salute of a wave and went out the gate.

Penny was looking at the concrete in the tubs, and it took her a while to realise Izzy was staring at her.

"What?" she said.

"Did you just invite Aubrey to Briony and Ross's wedding?"

"No. I was just... just checking my options," she said, her cheeks flushing with embarrassment

18

Izzy had taken yards of tulle, the most delicate net fabric, and used more of it in the construction of the swan dress than she would have imagined possible. She had found that it created a pleasing effect if she gathered strips tightly and layered them as closely as she could, but at the same time she felt as if she were drowning in tulle. For a garment that would look so light and airy, it contained a surprising density of fabric. She'd looked back on photographs of Bjork at the Oscars and she could see why so many of the pictures featured the singer burying her arms in the cloudy mass of her skirt. Izzy could imagine it might feel a little like throwing yourself into a giant pile of leaves.

"We will need to order some more tulle," she shouted to Penny, "I can see I'm going to use more or less all of this."

Penny wandered over. "Can we look at it on the mannequin?" she asked.

"Good idea," said Izzy. She took a break from machining

on the layers and slipped it over the mannequin's head. "I'll hold it in place with some pins."

Once it was secured into place, she stepped back.

"It's looking stunning," said Penny. "Is it as heavy as you feared?"

Izzy nodded. "I'm making a foundation to support it from underneath. We should get Monica in to make sure that's right."

"So, if we time it right, she can try on the bodysuit and the foundation together," said Penny. "Will tomorrow work?"

"Think so," said Izzy.

"It will be all the boring bits we're getting her to try on, I hope she's not put off the idea," said Penny thoughtfully.

Izzy considered that. Monica was not a typical customer in that respect. Was there a chance that she might lose enthusiasm for the project and decide not to wear the dress at all, going to the wedding in her jeans instead? "Maybe we fix up the mannequin for when she comes in so that she can see the effect that the final dress will have?"

"Great idea," said Penny.

Izzy checked the time. "Can't stay long. Got a Frambeat Gazette meeting and Marcin and I are off out on a date this afternoon. I told him that you thought dates should be a bit more active."

"You didn't! Did you? Why did you?"

"He said he had another plan."

"What is it?"

"He said we would do something exhilarating, something to make me breathless."

"But he didn't say what?"

"Um. No. I think it requires specialised equipment."

"You really shouldn't be telling your boyfriend my opinions of your date activities," said Penny, apparently mortified.

"Maybe you should go on a few more dates yourself and then we can reciprocate."

"In my own sweet time," said Penny.

"You have an invite to a wedding in exactly two weeks. Pick someone. Ask them."

In the end, Izzy pretty much had to run to get to the newspaper editorial meeting. Izzy was part of the team that produced the free Frambeat Gazette. The four of them met, as always, in the community room of the Millers Field sheltered accommodation.

Glenmore Wilson presided over their meeting and coughed when Izzy turned up, indicating that she was late.

"What?" said Izzy. "You hadn't even started."

"We have a lot to get through. We have an important story in the shape of that woman who died at the Letheringham Hotel."

"It's certainly very sad," said Izzy.

"I believe we have an exclusive, Annalise?"

"I'm not sure I would describe it quite like that," said Annalise the librarian, who never enjoyed the limelight. "It's just that Catriona once gave me her recipe for ginger cake."

"Sounds like an exclusive to me!" declared Glenmore. "We will print it alongside the touching tributes that young Tariq will gather from her friends and colleagues."

"I wondered if we could focus on the green energy angle," said Tariq.

"Green energy?" asked Glenmore.

Tariq had joined the Frambeat Gazette as a work experience activity while he was doing a media-related qualification at the university in Ipswich. He'd now been on the newspaper team for over a year. Izzy guessed that he had another income from somewhere else, because the decidedly amateur Frambeat Gazette wasn't paying anyone anything. Nonetheless, Tariq sometimes acted like he was a hard-bitten investigative reporter from the golden age of newspaper journalism.

"Catriona Wallerton drowned in the concrete foundations of a soon-to-be installed wind turbine," he said. "Was this some sort of ecological protest on her part?"

"For or against wind turbines?" said Annalise, confused.

"Well, I suppose, it could be either," said Tariq. "Certainly, her behaviour has raised awareness of the issue. It's good that the hotel is looking at renewable energy resources."

"I wouldn't be surprised if my environmentally conscious cousin Olivia hadn't bullied the events manager there into getting one installed," said Izzy, off-handedly.

"Oh, you know the people there?" said Glenmore.

"The events manager went to the same school as a lot of us. Briony seems to be calling in all manner of favours to get this wedding organised. The hotel, the flowers, the cake."

"And you knew Cat," added Glenmore.

"Not really. Only as the cake shop owner. It's been years since I spent much time with her."

"Other than the hen party, of course. You were there, weren't you?" asked Tariq, his eyes lit up in the way they did when he thought he'd caught the scent of a Pullitzer prize or a knighthood for amazing journalism or whatever it was that went through his mind. Izzy respected Tariq's enthusiasm, but found it irritating when it was directed at her.

"I was there but I don't think I can tell you anything meaningful. Go to the bakery and get some quotes from there."

Glenmore made a small harrumphing noise and moved on to the next matter on the agenda. There was a sequence of buzzes from Izzy's phone, text messages arriving in quick succession.

There was a direct message from Marcin. I'VE GOT THE HARNESSES. READY WHEN YOU ARE. With the message was a selfie of Marcin outside, along with a complicated arrangement of leather straps and buckles.

Izzy's mind spun with the possibilities of what that equipment might be used for.

There was also a message from Briony Hart. It had the non-specific tone of a message written to be sent to a large number of people. There were no names, no personal touches.

WE'RE HAVING DRINKS TOMORROW NIGHT IN MEMORY OF CATRIONA. A CHANCE TO RAISE A GLASS BEFORE THE WEDDING WEEKEND. IT'S AT THE BAR AT LETHERINGHAM HALL FROM EIGHT. DRESS CODE IS SMART CASUAL.

Well, that was interesting, she thought, staring at her phone so intently that she failed to realise that Glenmore was talking to her.

"Perhaps you're looking at a message from her now!" said Glenmore sternly.

"Huh?" said Izzy and raised her head.

"Madame Zelda," said Glenmore.

"What I —?"

"Glenmore was asking if Madame Zelda was up to date with her horoscopes column," explained Annalise helpfully.

"Yes. She will be. It's all in hand," said Izzy. "A lot of work goes into that column, it can't be rushed you know, there are charts to prepare and various sources to consult."

Tariq looked as if he was about to burst. "But surely Izzy just makes them up? Everyone knows there's no such person as —"

"Shush, Tariq!" said Annalise, shocked. She gave a light cough. "Biscuit anyone?"

They all tucked in. Everyone on the Frambeat Gazette team enjoyed a biscuit with their cup of tea.

19

At nightfall, Penny hurried upstairs to her flat to get straight under some warming blankets. Monty scampered at her heels, and once she was in her comfy armchair with a blanket and a hot water bottle on her lap, leapt up and snuggled in beside her. For a small dog, he seemed to enjoy taking up a lot of room.

She had a text message and a missed call on her phone.

The missed call was from Oscar. The text message was from Izzy, and said, Drinks at Letheringham Hall tomorrow night in memory of Cat. You should come.

Penny sent Izzy a message saying that she would come and asking how the date with Marcin had been. Then she called Oscar.

"Ah, hello," he said with surprising energy as he picked up.

"Sorry, I didn't notice your call earlier," she said.

"I'm sure you were doing something important."

"Yes. I had just popped out to put another brick in the concrete."

He hesitated. "That's either a delightful euphemism or a quaint rural practice I'm entirely unaware of."

"If I told you that we were trying to work out how quickly a body can sink in cement, would that help?"

"Not at all," he said. "Just makes it sound more intriguing."

"Oh, it's all go here in Fram," said Penny. "Dead bodies and wacky experiments. I can't imagine it holds a candle to the social whirl of London. At another party tonight?"

"No, not at all. I've actually just returned from an interesting dinner. You remember the friend of a friend who said I should be working for this company in New York?"

"Yes?"

"Well, I have just enjoyed a seafood linguine and a carafe of palatable wine with said friend of a friend. She's a lecturer in fashion at Kingston University."

Penny's stomach did something funny at Oscar's use of the word 'she'. Penny did not at all consider herself to be the jealous type and she knew full well that Oscar had female friends. How could one work in fashion and not have female friends? Nonetheless, she momentarily recoiled physically upon hearing that Oscar — *her* Oscar — was enjoying dinners out with a female fashion lecturer.

"A business dinner, then?" she asked, aware that the implied question was clumsy.

"I don't know about that," said Oscar. "Emily, the friend of a friend, perhaps made her international connections sound a bigger deal than they really were. Like so many people in the industry, she can be prone to exaggeration. I don't think I'll be hearing from any American fabric companies any time soon. No, I think she was more interested in me."

"Oh?" Penny's stomach did a double flip this time, and not in a good way.

She couldn't tell if he had heard or understood the tone of her voice, but he laughed. "Oh, it's nice to be the centre of attention now and again. We talked fabrics all afternoon. The other diners must have thought we were very dull, but you know how passionate I get about design."

"I... I do."

"Anyway, how goes the construction of the swan dress? Actually, Emily studied at St Martin's in London with Marjan Pejoski, the designer of Bjork's original dress."

"Oh, is that so?" said Penny without enthusiasm.

She gave Oscar a rundown of the recent dress developments, including Izzy's off-the-wall plan to put a camera in the swan head for photographic purposes. But her heart wasn't in the conversation any more. She felt an unjustified annoyance with Oscar and a desire to just stop things dead. Perhaps she could have asked Oscar to be her plus-one to the wedding there and then, challenged any hold this Emily had over him. But instead she harboured a feeling of annoyance which swiftly became annoyance at herself for foolishly thinking she had any hold over Oscar's life and his choices, annoyance that she couldn't make any firm choices for herself.

She ended the conversation as quickly as possible and

made an effort to sound honestly warm and friendly in her goodbyes before hanging up.

"Well, that was rotten," she told Monty. "He's out eating posh pasta with a beautiful fashion lecturer called Emily and I'm stuck here with you."

Monty yawned loudly. She tousled his fur. There was a reply message from Izzy. Penny had asked her what the date had been like. Izzy had replied, W ONDERFUL! E XHAUSTING! and then followed that with a litter of emojis. Such messages did not make Penny feel any better about herself.

20

On Sunday morning, Izzy came into Cozy Craft for a few hours after church to help Penny with a plan for the spring season. It was heartening to imagine the days slowly getting longer and the temperature rising a little. It seemed unimaginable to wear lightweight clothing when the weather was so cold, but they had to prepare workshops, fabric collections and sewing patterns for people to start sewing their summer outfits in a matter of weeks.

Penny couldn't help noticing that Izzy had a larger than usual smile on her face.

"Why are you grinning like that?" she asked. "You're bordering on manic, and it's a little bit alarming if I'm honest."

"Our date yesterday," said Izzy. "Best time ever. You will never guess what we did."

"Erm—" Penny had not the faintest idea. Something

wonderful, something exhausting, something involving complicated harnesses…

"No, you literally will never guess," said Izzy, "so I'll have to tell you. Husky sledding."

Penny nodded. "Husky sledding, right." She shook her head in confusion. "But it hasn't snowed."

"No," agreed Izzy, "but Marcin has a rig that's like a cross between a trolley and bicycle."

"I see. Does he also have some huskies?"

"Of course. He has six dogs. Three of them are huskies. He drove out to Rendlesham Forest and I did some sledding with all three pulling me. It was amazing. I felt like I was flying! They run and turn when you tell them to." Izzy was leaning left and right as she relived the experience. She pulled out a picture to show Penny.

"What? That is quite an insubstantial thing. I imagined something like Santa's sleigh, but this is more like a unicycle with ideas above its station."

"That's part of the magic. It's just you and the dogs whooshing along. Marcin looks amazing when he drives the dogs, like some sort of conquering hero. Although he looked a bit less heroic when he lost one of his gloves and had to spend twenty minutes in the bushes failing to find it."

"Well I'm so glad you had fun." Penny grappled for more to say, but the dates that Izzy and Marcin were enjoying seemed so far removed from Penny's own idea of a date that she struggled to picture them. "So you went round to his place, got the huskies and the sled and then went out riding? Did you do anything else?"

"Of course! When we were out, we both had a few sips of krupnik."

"That's the honey vodka stuff, is it?"

"Marcin says that the enjoyment of food and drink often depends on the context, so he wanted me to try some while we were out in the cold and the dark. He said the rush of air from riding the sled would enhance the warm feeling of swallowing a sweet and powerful liqueur. I think he was right, it was amazing."

"Huh." It sounded as if the shared experience had made quite a mark on Izzy. Penny was delighted for her, and delighted that Marcin seemed to be someone who could make a connection with Izzy's fun side, and not at all jealous or angry with herself for failing to make any sort of connections with anyone at all.

"Hey, Aubrey's coming," said Izzy. "Let's see what he thinks about our spring workshop plan."

Izzy whisked open the door and ushered Aubrey inside. "Aubrey, good. Come in."

"Er, good morning," he said. He had a wrapped parcel under his arm.

"Now, a question!" said Izzy. "A two hour Saturday morning workshop to plan an outfit. Would people go for it?"

"Erm..." Aubrey looked terrified.

"I'm not sure that Aubrey is our target market," said Penny. "Aubrey, Izzy's thinking is that we might attract a broader audience, people who aren't interested in sewing, but who might enjoy the chance to flick through magazines, identify gaps in their wardrobe and swap ideas about how to fill their upcoming outfit needs."

"Sounds great," said Aubrey. "You should give it a try."

"Righto, I'll pencil it in for March or April," said Penny, tapping at the laptop.

"I have something for you," said Aubrey, handing Penny the parcel. It was wrapped in flowery paper. "You can open it now."

Penny looked at his face and tried to read what might be going on. "I, er. What's the occasion, Aubrey?"

"It's another little something to keep you warm. You did say it was still cold in your rooms."

"Oh, I see. Let's have a look." Penny pulled off the paper and found a large folded garment inside. It was made from pink fleece and the top was visible, with a high neck and large buttons. She shook it out to see the rest of it. It was long, very long. She held it up against her body.

"Oh good, it's just the right length," said Aubrey. "I had to guess."

By 'just the right length' he meant that it went from just under her chin to the floor. "Full length, huh? It's a house coat, isn't it?"

"It is! You can wear it in your flat as an extra layer. It looks very warm."

"It does," said Penny. The house coat might as well have been a medieval queen's furry robes, bright pink queenly robes.

"That will keep you toasty," said Izzy. Her eyes were filled with mirth, but she kept a straight face.

"Thank you, this is a very thoughtful gift, Aubrey," said Penny. She was never going to wear this hideous garment, but she didn't need to crush him.

He smiled warmly. "That's great. Hope it helps. I've also come round to see how your concrete is doing. Did you put extra bricks in?"

"Just as instructed," said Penny.

"Shall we take a look, then?"

"Give us a minute. We'll be right round."

Aubrey stepped outside. Penny turned to Izzy as soon as he was gone, the hideous house coat bunched in her hands. "What on earth am I going to do with this? It's so horrible and old-fashioned."

"It might fit Nanna Lem if we take up the hem a bit," said Izzy.

"Nanna Lem is a stylish woman, she would hate this as much as I do," said Penny. "I'll take it to the charity shop."

"You can't take it to one in Fram, he might see it," Izzy pointed out.

"Fine." Penny rolled her eyes in frustration. "I will save it until I go somewhere else and then I will donate it to a charity shop far, far away."

"He means well," Izzy pointed out.

"I guess."

"He *genuinely* cares."

Penny sighed. "Of course he does. It's truly thoughtful."

Together, with coats on against the cold, the cousins went round the back of the shops to the Cozy Craft back yard where Aubrey crouched, inspecting the tubs of poured concrete. He jammed the tip of a rusted trowel in one. With force applied, it sank in a few inches.

"Even now it's not entirely dry," he said, "but look."

He pointed at two of the tubs. "This is where I put a brick

in when we first poured it. That one disappeared completely. This — twelve hours later? — has left a gloopy swirl of a clue on the surface. But then these…"

The brick representing Saturday evening had indeed sunk several inches, but the stiffening cement had not closed over the top of it.

"That was like the footprints we saw on the removed chunks," said Izzy.

"So, at that time, something could sink in slowly but wouldn't be automatically covered," he said.

"So that means," said Penny and tried to work out what that meant. "So, that means Cat would have had to have been pushed down into the concrete. Or had fresh concrete poured over her."

"Either way, that accident's not an accident," said Izzy.

"Suicide, then," said Aubrey.

"Or murder," said Penny.

Aubrey stood and the three of them solemnly considered the implications.

"There's a drinks thing at Letheringham Hall this afternoon," said Izzy. "I had a text from Briony. All of us who were there last weekend are invited. Reading between the lines, I think she wants to get all the grieving and shoe-gazing done and out of the way before the big day in a fortnight's time."

"Makes sense," said Aubrey. "Well, it does. Are you going to go?"

"I think we should all go," said Izzy.

"All of us?" said Aubrey.

Penny nodded in agreement. "If Cat was murdered then

this is a legitimate chance to speak to the last people who saw her alive."

"I'm not a crime solving detective," said Aubrey.

"No. You're the loose cannon thrown into the mix. Possibly the only person there who isn't a suspect."

"Oh, heck. There are suspects now?"

"I don't think Cat was a universally loved woman," said Izzy. "Dress code for the event is smart casual."

Aubrey groaned. "I never know what that means."

"It means dress casually but with some formal elements," said Izzy.

"Look, I have work wear, I have jeans and T-shirts and I have two suits — one for weddings, one for funerals."

"Maybe this is the gap in your wardrobe that needs addressing with a two hour workshop in the spring," Penny pointed out, with a smile.

21

Climbing out of Aubrey's van at Letheringham Hall, Izzy decided that Aubrey had made a respectable effort at smart casual. Despite his claimed wardrobe limitations, he had found a pair of light coloured trousers, a pastel polo shirt and a suit jacket that didn't look terrible with the ensemble.

"And my job is to make small talk while you grill the suspects, huh?" he asked.

"Or just enjoy the free canapés," said Penny.

"Are there going to be canapés?" said Izzy.

"Oh, I hope so."

They hurried inside. The broad reception area beneath the sweeping wooden staircase at the centre of the hall was dotted with comfy chairs, several clustered around open fireplaces that had been lit to ward off the cold. Izzy warmed her hands for a moment, considered where the bar might be in a place like this and then, with more optimism than knowledge, set off towards the rear of the building. Soon, in a side room not far from the orangery wedding venue, they found some familiar faces in a library room that had been converted into a bar.

The guests from the hen night were all there, and a few other figures besides.

Izzy nudged Penny. "That's Ross Blowers. The groom."

Penny looked at the man chatting to Shirley Hart. "Monica's brother," she said. "The family resemblance is obvious."

Whether it was genetics or farming life, there was something about Ross that he shared with his sister, a thoroughly dependable look, almost as if a no-nonsense attitude could be baked into someone's physical appearance.

Many of the others were gathered in a loose circle in the centre of the room. A tray of drinks had been brought over.

"And there are indeed canapés," said Penny with a nod.

"I'm glad I came," said Aubrey, lightly.

Izzy caught Briony's eye and waved. Briony waved back cheerily, seemed to remember herself and then pulled a cartoonish sad face and beckoned her over.

"So glad you could make it. Such a sad time."

"Thanks for the invite," said Izzy. She looked at the circle of friends and associates. "I've brought my cousin, Penny. I think most of you know her. And this is Aubrey. He's our…"

"I'm like an emotional support animal," said Aubrey. "You know, like the ones rich people take on planes. Except I'm also a painter and decorator."

There were dutiful smiles, and drinks were handed out.

"Don't I know that man over there?" Izzy heard Aubrey say to Penny.

"Gavin Bellforth, the florist," said Penny.

"Of course. We were in the same school rugby team."

"You were a rugby player?"

"Not my thing, really, but I was a big lad and my PE teacher wouldn't take no for an answer."

Izzy glanced at Gavin Bellforth. He was standing dutifully and silently behind Olivia, his other half. Olivia saw her looking their way.

"We were just saying what a wonderful person Cat was," she said.

"Yes. It's still very shocking," replied Izzy, wondering if and when she would feel compelled to share their theory that Cat was murdered.

"A very helpful person," added Olivia. "Insisted on helping with Briony's wedding."

"She did insist," said Briony.

"Practically bullied her way to the heart of it," said Shirley, coming through to get a second glass.

"But very giving," said Olivia. "Shop neighbours with Gavin here. Cat was always popping in to help him."

Behind her, Gavin nodded dutifully.

"She made the wedding cake, didn't she?" said Penny. "We always like Wallerton's cakes. Do you, er, do you have the cake?"

"Mostly done," Briony told her. "The team at the shop are finishing off the icing. A traditional three-tier wedding cake. I have a photo here somewhere..." She got out a phone.

"Isn't it unlucky to see the cake before the day?"

"I think you're thinking of the bride's dress," said Dr Denise.

Penny went over to look at Briony's picture of the cake on her phone.

Shirley, who had probably seen pictures of the cake many times, sidled over to Izzy.

"It's good that we're all able to say our, well, not quite fond farewells, I suppose, but still, to share our memories of Cat. Thought now would be a good time, rather than on Briony's happy day."

"Indeed," said Izzy. "I suppose there will be a funeral soon."

"Not for a while. The coroners will need to release the body first," said Denise. "In cases of unusual or unexpected deaths there may have to be an inquest."

"Oh, they think it's unusual?" said Shirley.

"She drowned in cement," Denise pointed out.

"It's quite hard to drown in cement," said Aubrey, and might have gone on to explain if Shirley hadn't spoken first.

"I suppose it doesn't matter," said the mother of the bride and then immediately felt the need to clarify her odd remark. "I mean, her mum is her only family and the poor old dear doesn't seem to know what day it is half the time. Maybe having Cat for a daughter drove her mad. I'll say this much for Cat, though. She paid for her mum's place at that Miller's Field place. Not every child is that caring."

Denise grunted. It was odd how a single noise could convey such a depth of contempt, but Denise managed it somehow.

"You think differently?" said Shirley.

Denise held her wine glass in both hands and pulled a tight-lipped expression. "I often find that as parents get older and the burden of care shifts from one generation to the next, finances become blurred."

"Well, that's a flaming cryptic remark," said Shirley and then laughed. "But who'd expect different from a doctor? They often talk like they're a different species."

"We try not to," said Denise.

"Actually, since you're a doctor, I wonder if I could talk to you about this rash I've been getting."

As Shirley bodily dragged her away, Denise shot Izzy and Aubrey a 'See what I have to put up with?' look. Izzy smiled in sympathy and tried to avoid laughing out loud.

22

Drinks flowed and platters of finger food were brought in to the bar. Penny knew about half the people in the place and recognised many of the others from social cliques at school she definitely hadn't belonged to.

She thought it was funny how, even in a light and informal setting like this, the people were splitting off into distinct groups, like orbiting planets in a social solar system. There was definitely a core of women, the bride and her mother and a few friends, laughing and talking raucously. Gavin hung close to that group, but only because he was pulled in by the silent gravitational force of his girlfriend, Olivia. Further out, though, quieter groups had formed. She saw Aubrey chatting to Ross and Monica Blowers beneath a framed hunting print by the fireplace. Something about the air of them suggested they were glad to be further away from the noisy social heart of the event. She wondered what the decorator, the farmer and the Land Rover nut might be talking about. Something eminently practical and sensible, she thought.

She was about to go over and find out when she heard Shirley Hart say the words, "Of course, Cat broke Briony's leg, and I don't think I'll ever forgive her for that."

Given recent events, Penny couldn't let a remark like that go ignored. She moved closer to the central group of women.

"Mother," said Briony testily. "She did not break my leg. I broke my leg. My own stupid fault."

Olivia smiled. "This was the accident you had at the Halloween party when we were — what? — seventeen? Eighteen?"

"She was sixteen, as well you know," said Shirley. "Her father and I were away for the weekend."

"Oh, yes."

"And *someone* insisted you have a party," said Shirley, her tone making it perfectly clear that the *someone* in question was Catriona Wallerton.

"In all honesty, it was a great party," Briony smiled. "I think it had just been after Cat's birthday and her mum had refused to allow her a party of her own."

"That poor woman had had enough of Cat's shenanigans, that's why," said Shirley.

"God, we were all there, weren't we?" said Olivia, her eyes alight with the joy of nostalgia. "Hey, Izzy, were you at that Halloween party where Briony broke her leg?"

Izzy, engaged in conversation with Denise, looked up. "At the beginning. I left early."

"We were all there," said Denise. "In fact, Gavin, weren't you going out with Cat at the time?"

There was a mixture of gasps of amusement and furtive glances, none more furtive and embarrassed than those given by Gavin Bellforth. It seemed to Penny that Gavin found acting as Olivia's silent shadow more than enough social interaction. Being made the centre of attention and of conversation was far beyond what he craved.

"It was a long time ago," he mumbled into his glass.

"Childhood sweethearts, I recall," said Shirley.

"In fact, Gavin and Cat split up that night," said Olivia primly. "And not long after, we two became an item. How many years is it now?"

Gavin mumbled and nodded.

"Perhaps we might be the next to get hitched," said Olivia. "Once all this business is done and dusted."

There was clatter as a member of hotel staff almost collided with the door as he brought in more food.

"Done and dusted?" said Briony. "My wedding?"

"You know what I mean!" said Olivia, refusing to be apologetic. "In fact, I think this wedding is going to be so amazing, we might have to use Letheringham Hall for our own wedding. What do you think, James? Can you squeeze another wedding in somewhere?"

The member of staff set down the latest platter of beige buffet things and turned with a smile. "Here I am, events manager, waiter and walking appointments calendar. Yes! I'm sure we can, Olivia. When would you like me to squeeze it in?"

"Well, someone has to propose first," Olivia pointed out.

"If you insist," said James and, with a goofy look, pretended to get down on one knee before 'realising' his mistake and getting up again.

Penny gestured between the hotel guy, James, and the women. "Oh, you all know each other too?"

"Same school year. Old friends," said Briony.

"James and I were inseparable mates," added Olivia.

"And were you at this Halloween party when my girl got her leg broken?" asked Shirley, unwilling to let the matter go.

"Was I there?" replied James with a rueful smile. "I was the one who went in the ambulance with her to hospital."

This drew laughs from several of them. There was a tug on Penny's arm. It was Izzy. She gestured for her to come over and join Aubrey and Denise by the fire.

"Aubrey shared our drowning in concrete theory with Denise," Izzy said in a low, conspiratorial voice.

"Oh, did he?"

"He's quite right," said Denise. "It really doesn't add up."

"You think she was murdered?" said Penny.

"*You* think she was murdered?" Denise came back at her.

"We had discussed the drowning problem but hadn't quite got round to the possibility of murder," said Izzy.

"I know the accident seems improbable..."

"Crazy improbable," said Aubrey.

"I thought that Aubrey and I might go down to the lake and compare our experimental data with the facts on the ground," said Izzy.

"Did you just use the phrase 'experimental data' in relation to some bricks in some tubs, Izzy?" asked Penny. "Shall I come?"

"We can't all go. It will look weird."

"Well, I'm coming," said Denise. "This theory sounds exciting. Besides..." She looked across at the bride and her chatting friends. "This isn't exactly my scene."

"So, I'm going to stay here and keep up the social expectations of my absent friends," Penny tutted.

"That's the spirit," said Izzy, patting her arm, and then slipped out of the room with Aubrey and Denise.

Penny selected a fresh glass of wine from the table. She would need one if she was to hold the fort with Izzy's old chums. She saw the hotel guy, James, and raised her glass to him.

"You have a lovely venue here," she said. "So you were in the same school year as Briony and Izzy and this lot?"

"These fine people were my friends at secondary. I think I sat next to Olivia in half my subjects."

"I think you were perhaps a bit sweet on me," said Olivia, overhearing the conversation.

James laughed. "I don't think I'd quite put it like that."

Penny turned to Olivia. "So, what was this thing about a broken leg and a party?"

James moved off to gather empty plates and glasses.

"Halloween. Maybe a dozen of us round at Briony's parents' place."

"Ha! Seventy more like!" said Shirley loudly. "No point lying about it years after the event."

"Okay, so maybe thirty people," said Briony. "And, yes, maybe the whole thing had been Cat's idea."

"I knew it!"

"The cheap cider flowed like water," said Olivia. "We

were teenagers and there really isn't much for teenagers to do in a town like Fram, so we danced and we drank. Some people came in fancy dress. And Cat —" A smile of remembrance crossed her face. "Of course, that was why Izzy left early."

"Did she?" said Briony.

"You remember the dress that Cat wore, don't you?" said Olivia. "I think that probably killed Izzy's friendship with her. I'm surprised Izzy never tried to get revenge on her for that."

23

"Where are you three off to?"

Izzy stopped on the gravel driveway and turned. Monica stood on the steps of Letheringham Hall.

"Er, we're just going to go down to the lodges and the lake to check something out," said Izzy.

"Izzy thinks Cat was murdered," Denise called out, far too loudly.

Monica nodded slowly, chin up, chin down, as if this was an unusual notion, but not a mad one.

"It's dark down there," she said, looking to the descending gloom of the winter night. "How are you going to see without proper torches?"

"I've got my phone," said Izzy.

Monica produced a strap-on head torch from her pocket and put it on. It produced a tight bright beam.

"You wouldn't happen to have a spare?" asked Denise.

"I might have," said Monica, producing another.

Together, the four of them made their way down the path towards the lodges. Not far down the path, the security lights on tall poles came on, clearly illuminating the way ahead.

"So, you're one of the bridesmaids?" Aubrey asked Denise.

"Definitely the third bridesmaid," said Denise. "Olivia and Briony have been bosom buddies for years. They own a handmade soap company together." She grunted in derisory laughter. "Then Cat became a bridesmaid. Shirley's not wrong that she bullied Briony into giving her that role. I think I was then asked to join, to sort of rectify the balance between the good bridesmaids and the evil bridesmaid."

"And you're not a fan of handmade soap?"

"I have no problem with handmade soap or *artisanal* soap as I believe they call it. We live in an age where so much business is soaked up by big impersonal corporations. Supporting the little guy is great but it's... ugh." She struggled to find the words.

"Some people who handcraft things, don't exactly put much *craft* into it," Izzy said. "I know exactly what Denise means. Glitter and ribbons do not a handicraft make."

"Right," agreed Denise. "You can probably make excellent handmade soap. Rendering the fat or whatever it is and mixing in the lye and adding carefully selected scents and colours. You can do all that."

"Or...?" said Aubrey.

"You can take pre-existing soap from the supermarket shelves, mush it down, add a sprig of rosemary or whatever and then remould it and repackage it and sell it as something it isn't for five times the price."

"Ah, I see."

"It's just a tax on gullible new age vegetarian yummy mummies," said Denise and then stopped. "I have had two glasses of wine. I might be speaking a little harshly."

"I didn't know you had problems with vegetarians."

"I use carbolic soap," added Monica. "Always have. Always will. Antiseptic qualities and that lovely leather smell."

"This was where I found Cat's shoe," said Izzy, shining a light on a bench. "It was there when I woke up and gone again when Monica and I came by later."

They walked down into the network of paths and neat borders that connected the closely arranged lodges. They were all dark. There were no guests staying there at the moment.

"This was Cat's lodge here," said Izzy, shining a light.

"Are you sure?" asked Denise.

Izzy reconsidered. "Mine, yours, Olivia's, Cat's."

Denise frowned and turned around. "But which way is east?"

It was dark and there was no telling the direction from the sun. As if to underscore the point, the security lights on the path went out and, but for their torches and phones and the pale glow of the solar lights in the garden borders, they were in darkness.

Izzy walked over to Cat's lodge and, more to prompt her own thoughts than anything, rattled the doorknob.

"We all locked our doors that night," she said. "We each had our own key."

"We did," agreed Monica.

Izzy turned. "If Cat was murdered, or if someone else was involved in her death, then they either broke in and killed her or enticed her out and killed her."

"Or she was just out and about and happened to bump into an axe-wielding murderer," said Denise.

"Did they do it with an axe?" asked Monica.

"No. Denise is being silly," said Izzy.

"The killer would have had to have come down this path," said Denise and moved towards the path to the main hall. The security lights came on.

"If they did, they would have set off the lights," said Aubrey.

"We were dead drunk and fast asleep," said Denise.

Izzy shook her head and pointed at one of the security lights. "That one shone right into my bedroom, right through the curtains. Even in sleep, I would have noticed that."

"Well, that's not possible," said Denise, "because there's just no other way round."

She began exploring round the side of the lodge nearest the path. Aubrey moved round the other side. Izzy could see the point Denise was testing. The trees and the green mesh fence that defined the borders of the woods here closed in behind the lodges at both ends of the path, both down to the lake and up to Letheringham Hall. It could well be the case that there was no way to the lodges without coming directly down the path.

There was an 'oof' and a scuffle from Aubrey's direction. Izzy whirled round with her phone torch.

"Just kicked something," he said from the darkness.

"Is it a blood-stained axe?" called Monica.

"No one did anything with an axe," Izzy reminded her.

Denise came back round, brushing leaf mould from her hands. "There's no way through that way. The killer had to come down that path."

"Similarly blocked that way," said Aubrey, coming back into the torchlight, with a small and damp cardboard box in his hand.

"What's that?" said Denise.

"A discarded box of chocolates." He turned them over. "Ah, Raw Chocolate Company. It's vegan. Probably not your sort of thing, Denise."

"I'm not saying I hate vegans —" Denise began but Izzy couldn't contain the contradictions in her mind.

"I would have seen the security light come on," she insisted. "It was, like, laser bright. Maybe the killer found another way into this area. Perhaps came up from the lake."

"In the dark? In the middle of the night?" said Monica. "Or there's a more obvious explanation."

"Really?"

Monica shrugged. "The killer was already here when we went to bed."

"Like lurking in the bushes?" said Denise.

"Perhaps, or even simpler..." She looked from person to person, her headtorch shining on them in turn. "Cat's killer was one of the people staying here in these lodges."

Izzy felt a cold shiver go down her spine, and it might

have been the chill evening air, but it was an unpleasant sensation nonetheless.

"Cat opened her door to her killer because it was someone she knew." Monica directed her light at each of the lodges. "Me, Izzy, Denise, Olivia, Briony and Shirley. One of us killed Cat."

24

Briony was laughing out loud as she tried to tell Penny the story in the bar.

"So, you know Izzy has always been a sewing nerd. Yes, yes, I know she's managed to make something of a career out of it now but back then it was just an obsession. You know what I mean? So, it had been Cat's birthday and the two of them — fifteen, sixteen years old — were the best of friends, or at least they would hang around together, so Izzy had decided to make her friend a dress for her birthday. I suppose it was cheaper than going out to buy a proper present."

Penny bit her tongue and didn't point out that actually making someone a dress was both more time-consuming and more expensive than buying a dress off the rack at a high-street clothing store. It was one of the bugbears of the dressmaking profession. Penny occasionally contemplated putting up a sign in the shop to point this out to annoying customers.

"Izzy had made this thing, this dress, all flounces and puffed sleeves," said Briony. "Not quite a nightie but sort of the thing that a woman might wear in a period drama. It was not to everyone's tastes."

"I thought it was lovely," said Olivia.

"Well, yes," Briony conceded. "It was gorgeous, but it was not normal. I don't know if Cat could ever see herself wearing it in a *normal* situation and then it was the Halloween party at mine and I guess she just thought, wouldn't it be very in keeping with the Halloween vibe to turn up as a sort of zombie bride with a ripped, blood-spattered dress."

Penny nearly spat out her drink. "She ripped it up?!"

"It looked good," said Gavin.

They were the first proper words the big florist had spoken all evening. Olivia gave him a sharp look.

"The boyfriend obviously thought it looked good," said Briony.

"Cat came to the party having ripped up the dress Izzy made for her," said Penny. "I can see why Izzy left early."

"I'm surprised she didn't kill Cat, the hurt it must have caused," said Shirley, and then realised what she'd said and raised her glass. "Speaking no ill of the deceased, you understand."

"Cat was always one for thoughtless excesses, Mum," said Briony. "She came that night with Gavin and —"

"Plied you with drink no doubt," said Shirley.

Olivia jerked a thumb at Gavin. "This one here looked

old enough to buy alcohol. Came with a big box of Strongbow and enough WKDs to drown us all."

"I can't even look at one of them any more without feeling queasy," said Briony.

"And how did you come to break your leg?" Penny asked.

"We lived in a bungalow at the time," said Shirley. "A proper one. Not a granny bungalow. But it was easy enough to climb on the water butt at the back of the house and get onto the roof."

"Oh, a party on the roof," said Penny.

"We were young, stupid and having fun," said Briony. She paused, twirling her glass stem. "I suppose it doesn't matter now that Cat is dead."

"What doesn't matter?"

"We were drinking, that's true, but, um, Cat was already into her baking at that point."

"Yes? And?" said Shirley.

"She made some brownies."

Penny caught on long before Shirley did. Briony's mum was frowning furiously in incomprehension.

"With a special ingredient, Mrs Hart," Olivia said.

"Cannabis, Mum," said Briony.

Shirley's eyes went wide. "You were high?"

"Literally and metaphorically," Briony nodded. "I was dancing on the ceiling. The Sugababes or the Pussycat Dolls or whatever it was we were listening to that year and, yeah, I put my foot down on a bit of roof that just wasn't there and…"

Events manager James popped his head into the circle. "If it's any consolation, I think you were so high that you barely noticed you'd broken your leg when you hit the ground."

"Thank you very much, young man," snapped Shirley, utterly unconsoled. "A wonderful future in contemporary dance ruined."

"I was never going to be a dancer, Mum," Briony smiled.

"Cat thought the whole thing was hilarious, even when you were rolling around, crying," said Olivia. "I think that was when this big lunk here realised his girlfriend wasn't exactly the nicest person on the planet. James was there, always quick to help, and I asked him to go with Briony when the ambulance was called."

"Yes. Bravo to James," said Briony, looking round for the events manager to thank him, but he had left the room.

"Cat and Gavin had a big bust up while everyone else was scarpering home," said Olivia. "Simply presenting myself as a shoulder to cry on in the aftermath of that tragedy was enough to worm my way into this teddy bear's affections."

Gavin's cheeks flushed and he automatically put a loving hand on Olivia's shoulders.

"Life is full of funny twists and turns," said Briony.

Ross Blowers came over from the bar and spoke to his wife-to-be. "I'm sure we've lost some of our party somewhere. I've got no idea where Monica is."

"They've all just probably gone out for a crafty ciggie," said Penny, which was a rubbish excuse as she knew for a fact that Aubrey, Izzy and Monica did not smoke.

"I'm sure they're somewhere," said Briony swiftly. "Isn't it a shame that we don't have a colourful story about how we got together, like Olivia and Gavin have?"

"Who needs funny stories when you've got love?" replied Ross which, to Penny's ears, sounded both wonderfully sweet and horribly mawkish.

"Well, I suppose there is that," said Briony without enthusiasm.

There was movement at the door and a gaggle of new people came in. Briony gave a cheer of greeting and hurried over to hug them.

Penny couldn't help but think that for a gathering to fondly and sombrely remember the passing of Catriona Wallerton, hardly anyone seemed to be sad at her death or had much in the way of nice words to say about her.

25

By torchlight, the party of four investigators made their way down the winding woodland path to the lake.

"Look, just to clarify," Denise said, "I don't have anything against vegetarianism or veganism."

"And yet you spoke about veganism in the same breath and in the same tone as — what was it? — artisan soap making and new age hippy mums and whatever," said Aubrey.

"I..." Izzy heard Denise half-laugh, half-huff in the darkness. "I don't have to justify myself to you... Aubrey, is it? I take it you're a veggie then?"

"I think about what I eat," he said.

She did laugh at that, but in recognition rather than derision. "Yes, there. That's my problem with all that malarkey — if I do have a problem with it, which I don't. There are people who jump on faddy bandwagons without thinking about it."

"I'm not jumping on a bandwagon," he said.

"*Some* people," she countered firmly. "Some people read an article on the internet and the next thing you know they're drinking glasses of their own wee or doing complicated yoga poses to expose bits of their bodies to the sun where the sun was never meant to shi—"

Denise was interrupted by a loud honking sound, Aubrey gave a yell of surprise, and something furious and white flapped out of the darkness across their path.

"Blooming heck!" exclaimed Aubrey.

Monica shone her head torch on them. "Did one of you lot just walk into a nesting swan?"

"Might have done," said Aubrey, panting.

"We're at the lake edge," said Izzy. "Watch where you're treading. The concrete they removed is round this way."

Monica looked over the water. Torchlight reflected in sharp ribbons.

"If someone did kill Cat and took her over there, they'd have needed a boat to get to the island."

"We saw a rowing boat out there that morning, didn't we?" said Izzy. "Just floating by the island."

"But if someone took her out there, they'd need a boat to get back to shore."

Izzy thought about this. "Or they just got wet?"

"Two boats," said Aubrey. "A person rows one out, towing the other."

"In this made-up scenario, are we saying that Cat was alive at this point?" said Denise.

"I don't know," said Izzy.

"I mean, if I were Cat, I'd be kind of wondering. *Hey, why are we rowing out to this island in the middle of the night? And why do we need two boats?*"

"So, she was dead before," said Monica.

"Someone killed her up at the lodges and carried her down here? In the dark?"

"She wasn't exactly a big woman," Izzy pointed out.

"I could carry her, easy," said Monica.

"But the two boat thing..." said Izzy. "That sounds like the killer had this whole thing planned."

"Pre-meditated," said Denise.

"Someone planned to kill her," said Aubrey.

"Or," said Izzy. "She wasn't dead when she came down here. There were definitely footprints in the cement."

"The killer's footprints?" suggested Monica.

"Here," said Izzy and carefully crept down the grassy bank to where the lumps of dried concrete were gathered on the foreshore. "Footprints. Here."

She shone her light at the deep sloppy hole in the dried block of concrete.

Aubrey came over to her, passing something to Denise before he crouched down beside Izzy. "Here."

"Why are you carrying a box of soggy chocolates around with you?" said Denise.

"I'm not a litterbug," he said. "Don't eat them all at once."

"No fear."

"Because they're vegan?"

"Because you found them on the ground."

He inspected the footprint. "You know, you could take a plaster of Paris mould of that footprint."

"See what kind of shoe made it," said Monica. The light from her headtorch jiggled as she nodded in approval.

"And," said Denise, "it occurs to me, I have a colleague who is a police surgeon and she knows some folks at police headquarters in Ipswich, including the forensics people."

"I think we can get some plaster of Paris ourselves," said Izzy. "We don't need to get special forensic plaster."

"*I'm saying* that maybe the police have already done this," she said. "I could ask."

Izzy looked up at her. "You think the police think this is murder too?"

"Do *we* actually think this is murder?" said Monica. "Do we actually think one of us did it?"

"Cold-blooded murder..." Denise murmured thoughtfully.

Aubrey straightened up. "Speaking of cold, I think I'm losing the feeling in my feet. Maybe time to get back up to the hotel and a drink of something warming."

He wasn't wrong. The evening air was bone-chilling.

"Come on, gang," said Izzy. "Time to head back."

"Gang," smiled Denise. "Are we the mystery solving Famous Five now?"

"There's only four of us," said Monica.

"The Not-Particularly-Famous Four," said Denise.

As they made their way back round the lake, Aubrey hugged himself against the cold.

"How's Penny getting on in her cold flat?" he asked.

"She's trying to cope," said Izzy.

"She lives above your shop, doesn't she?" said Denise.

"It's quite an old and draughty building."

"I gave her something warm to wear about the house," said Aubrey.

"I have this super thick onesie," said Denise. "If I have a day where I'm not tending to ailments or injuries, I can spend the whole day just snuggled up in it, enjoying being in my own home."

"Sounds heavenly," said Aubrey.

Somehow they managed to startle the same nesting swan on the way back up to Letheringham Hall. It gave Aubrey a considerable fright again but at least it took their minds away from the deepening chill.

26

In the early part of the week following the drinks at Letheringham Hall, Penny worked on the bodysuit for Monica. The work was a distraction from the alarming implications of what they had both learned that weekend. The bodysuit was an interesting thing to sew because it was translucent. All of the seams had to be really neat as they would be visible from the outside. Even cutting out the fabric was different as the net was so slippery that she had to cut everything in a single layer for accuracy.

She used French seams on the straight seams, and then carefully finished the armholes by trimming one side of the seam allowance and folding the other side over.

"I really hope this doesn't need too much adjustment," she said to Izzy. "It would be quicker to make a whole new one than to unpick this."

"It probably would. That's one of the reasons we're just doing a small sample of the rhinestones, yeah?"

"Yes," said Penny. "I'll make some spangly star shapes on the sleeves."

These rhinestones were held in place with glue, so Penny packed the sleeves with some bubblewrap secured in a plastic bag in case of drips. Each stone was fixed in place with a dab of glue. "Isn't it surprising how well it glues onto the mesh, when you consider that a large part of mesh fabric is fresh air?" she said to Izzy.

Izzy came over to look. "Those look nice. Monica will love it. By the way, you should try that line on Oscar. Tell him we want a discount for the bits of the fabric that are fresh air."

Monty's lunchtime walk was a brisk jaunt. He sometimes enjoyed longer walks but this time Penny simply took him round a circuit of Market Hill. A clockwise circuit took in all the shops. He sniffed at the doorway of Thumbskill's games shop and at the door of Sal Butterwick's shop, freshly painted but not yet reopened, before they crossed over and worked their way down past the Crown Hotel and the only open bank that remained in the town. Down at the corner they came to Wallerton's bakery. The two younger women behind the counter had customers in the shop. Penny had no idea how a business continued to function practically when the owner was dead, but she guessed that the two women simply came in, opened up as usual and possibly just paid themselves out of the till. Two doors along was Bellforth's florist. The door was closed with a little adjustable clock sign on the door saying when Gavin would be back.

Cat had always been popping in to see Gavin, Olivia had said the other evening. It struck Penny as funny that Olivia would be so blasé about Gavin having his old girlfriend dropping in on him all the time. But it was a teenage romance in question, and such things perhaps shouldn't have much impact on adult lives. What people did as teenagers seemed to belong to a whole other life compared to what followed. Nonetheless, Penny thought, as she and Monty finished their circuit and walked back towards Cozy Craft, it was interesting that Cat and Gavin would probably have been drawn together even closer together by the preparations for the wedding, not that the florist and the cake maker had much reason to collaborate.

Izzy was bringing down cups of tea as Penny re-entered the shop.

"Cup of tea and three biscuits," said Izzy.

"Three?" said Penny.

"You, me and the young master here."

Monty sat in anticipation and gave a small yip to indicate he was ready. Izzy offered him a digestive biscuit, which he took politely and then savaged into crumbs that he then chased around the shop floor.

"Does your boyfriend know you give sugary human biscuits to our dog?" said Penny.

"There were only three left in the packet," said Izzy. "I couldn't leave just one."

"We're out of biscuits?"

"I think there's still some custard creams at the back of the cupboard."

Penny picked up her tea and luxuriated in the feel of the warm cup against her skin.

"Do you think that when people plan a wedding there's a

design theme that ties everything together?" she asked the air.

"I should hope so," said Izzy. "There would be if I planned a wedding."

"Hmmm. Even one between the cake design and floral displays?"

Izzy narrowed her eyes. "What are you thinking?"

"Wildly, wildly speculating. And I don't want to start a rumour."

"Understood," said Izzy. "Pure speculation, not starting a rumour. Are you about to put forward the notion that Cat and Gavin were having an affair?"

Penny grunted in amused agreement. "We have no evidence they were."

"None whatsoever. But it's an interesting thought. Cat and Olivia were sniping at each other on the hen night. The business with the bacon juices in the cornbread for one."

"Yes, exactly."

"But if you're suggesting that we have reason to suspect our cousin Olivia murdered Cat because Cat had her claws in Olivia's man… I don't know. I think we'd need to dig deeper."

"We would."

"But they were once boyfriend and girlfriend, and the gang all stayed close, socially like."

"It's worth thinking about."

"And speaking of potential boyfriends," said Izzy, "have you actually invited a man to come as your plus one to the wedding? It's a week on Saturday."

"I'm leaving it a bit late, aren't I?"

"Particularly if you want to make sure your guest's outfit co-ordinates with yours."

"I haven't even considered what I'm going to wear," said Penny honestly.

"So much to do, so little time," Izzy warned her.

27

On Wednesday morning, Izzy went over to Miller's Field to visit Nanna Lem. Sometimes it was hard to know when to visit Nanna Lem. For a woman in her ninth decade, she had a remarkably busy social life. The dancing she did was perhaps more sedate and her crafting activities were on a smaller scale than they once had been, but Izzy often found that a random visit to Nanna Lem's sheltered accommodation flat would end up interrupting some event or other.

Izzy stepped into the Millers Field reception area and almost collided with Denise Upton.

"Ooh," said Denise, "I'm glad I bumped into you."

Izzy gave her a suspicious look. "Do many people enjoy having their doctor say that they're glad to see them?"

Denise grinned. "I know. I only ever see people at their worst, in every sense. It's nice to be able to chat to people when they've not got a complaint."

She tilted her head towards the community room door. "Just dropped in on a regular to see how she is."

Izzy looked past and saw Irene Wallerton, Cat's mum, sat in a chair among a group of other residents.

"How's she taking it? Cat's death?"

"Oblivious to it," said Denise, and there was a strange glee in her voice. "One of the very few perks of memory loss, which is generally a cruel and vindictive business. If I had my way, I wouldn't even tell her about the funeral. Just pop Cat in a box and have done with." She pouted. "That sounded harsher than I intended."

"No," said Izzy, who did indeed think it sounded harsh. "It's nice to hear someone speaking frankly. You, um, said you were glad to see me."

"Oh, yes. Can I just say I thought it was an absolutely hoot playing Scooby Doo with you down by Letheringham Hall lake on Sunday?"

"I thought we were the Famous Five."

"Either way we're missing a dog. Anyway, Aubrey and I were messaging back and forth about it."

"Were you now?" said Izzy, and decided she'd squirrel that comment away for future contemplation.

"Yes. I mentioned that I have a friend who's police surgeon for the Suffolk constabulary. She said — this is all hush hush and on the QT, you understand?"

"I do."

"She said that she'd be able to have a look at the police files because there's a detective over in Woodbridge who owes her a favour, and it turns out the coroner has definitely raised some questions."

"Oh, that will be interesting," said Izzy.

"I'll pop into the shop when I know more," said Denise, turned up the collar of her coat and stepped out.

Ruminating on what Denise's contact might reveal, Izzy put her head inside the community room in case Nanna Lem was there, and indeed she was, among another group of residents.

"Come, come, I've got something for you," said Nanna Lem.

With nods and brief greetings for the others — those that were awake at least — Izzy slipped into the chair beside her grandma. The chair was high-backed but very soft. It was like a huge, cushioned hug. Izzy was surprised that more people didn't fall asleep in these chairs.

"Still knitting an endless scarf," observed Izzy.

"And these," said Nanna Lem. From beneath her nest-like mound of knitting she produced one, two, then three knitted white ovals. They were somewhat bigger than her fist and it took Izzy a moment or two to work out what they were.

"Have you knitted me some eggs, Nanna?" she asked.

"I have."

"Without wishing to appear rude, do you mind if I ask why?"

"For your swan dress, of course. I did some research. When that Icelandic singer wore her swan dress to the Oscars, she laid a number of fluffy eggs on the red carpet."

"Did she indeed?"

"And I thought it was such a strange and magical idea that maybe your customer might lay some eggs of her own."

"That's a very creative idea. Oh, I see, they're stretched around a polystyrene core?"

"You can get them from a craft shop," said Nanna Lem. "They're basically socks stretched and stitched around the support."

"They are lovely," said Izzy, taking them. "Although I would worry that if Monica starts laying eggs at Briony's wedding then people might think she's trying to upstage the bride."

Nanna Lem chuckled dryly. "If a woman turns up in a pure white swan dress to a traditional wedding, people might just get it into their heads that she's trying to upstage the bride even before she starts laying eggs, you know."

Izzy made a thoughtful noise. "The cake maker and bridesmaid already dead —"

"Two people are dead?"

"Sorry, no, same person, Nanna." She glanced across at Irene Wallerton on the other side of the room. Irene was gazing obliviously out at the white skies beyond the window. "With Cat Wallerton dead," Izzy said, "I think this wedding has experienced enough drama."

"Maybe fate doesn't want the wedding to go ahead."

"I don't know about fate. Although it's already been suggested to me that the happy couple are, well, that he loves her, but it's not required."

"Oh, is she being forced into it?" said Nanna Lem.

"No, Nanna! Nothing like that. I don't think so. I think the, er, cooler-hearted bride is the driving force behind the marriage."

"Well, there's nothing wrong with that," said the older

woman matter-of-factly.

"Really, Nanna?"

"Absolutely." There was a fixedness in her voice. "Love doesn't work how people think it does. Telly and movies and mushy romance novels have it all back to front. They tell us there's someone out there for us, our one true love, and that when we find them it's love at first sight and the finding of the person is the end of the story and that it's just your Happily Ever After after that. Love is not like that."

"No? I mean, when I first saw Marcin, I was sure I felt something —"

"That wasn't love, dear girl. That was something equally nice but it wasn't love. Only a mad person thinks love is this power from above, that you are given someone to love and must go and find them. In real life, you find someone and then you decide to love them. Love is built and sustained and manufactured over the course of years. Love isn't about finding two jigsaw pieces that fit. It's about two jigsaw pieces that don't quite fit but which lose their rough edges and sacrifice their odd bumps and lumps until they do fit."

"I don't know if that's sweet or horribly cynical, Nanna," said Izzy honestly.

Nanna Lem grinned and squeezed Izzy's arm. "I mean it helps if the young feller makes your knees tremble when you first see him. But trembling knees and butterflies in the tummy have to give way to something more substantial in the end. No, it don't matter if this bride doesn't really love her man yet as long as she's willing to put the effort in to learn to love him."

Seeing movement on the other side of the community

room, Izzy raised her head a little. Gavin Belforth was back in, sorting an arrangement in a vase. It wasn't exactly a floral arrangement, seemingly composed mostly out of twigs and sprigs of herbs, but there was something starkly beautiful about the arrangement, a genuine work of art.

"What if the person thinks they're with the wrong person?"

"People are weak and stupid and often fancy a bit of what they can't have. The grass is always greener and all that. Oh, there's people who are bad for each other and people who are just bad but never underestimate human weakness and stupidity. Take it from me."

Nanna Lem realised Izzy was looking past her, and adjusted her whole body with difficulty in the deep chair to look round and see Gavin.

"Oh? Is there a story there?" she asked.

"Not that I know," said Izzy. "Gavin and Cat used to be an item, back when they were teenagers."

"Oh, well it's never love when it comes to teenagers."

"And Gavin is with our Olivia now, and yet we were at this drinks thing on Sunday and, by Penny's account, it was open knowledge that Cat was always dropping into Gavin's shop."

"People are allowed to be friends with their exes," Nanna Lem pointed out. "And if he's going out with our Olivia and that whole crowd of girls bumps along together then it's no surprise he's going to be seeing Cat, is it?"

"True," said Izzy. She knew she sounded doubtful, but it wasn't because Nanna Lem's words didn't make sense. The idea that Gavin and Cat had been having an affair would give a potential motive for why Olivia might want to see Cat dead, or even Gavin himself if the affair had turned sour. Right now it was all fantasy and conjecture, with no substantiating evidence.

Gavin had bent slightly to talk to Irene Wallerton, and was gesturing to something outside the window. The woman seemed barely animated in reply, but nodded along as he talked.

"I think I'm going to talk to him," said Izzy, gathering up her clutch of woollen eggs.

"Are you going to make a fool of yourself and say something daft?" asked Nanna Lem.

"No. Why?"

"Just wondering if I need to get my phone out to take a commemorative photo."

Izzy tutted at her and got up. She tried to saunter casually over to Gavin and then realised she didn't know how to saunter casually, particularly with a small pile of knitted eggs in her arms, so she just walked over to Gavin. He was moving the third and final vase into the room.

"Those are nice, er, twigs," she said, pointing at his display.

"I could do an actual floral display," he replied. "But they would be imported flowers and I like to use local, native flora when I'm given the choice."

"Very environmentally conscious," Izzy nodded, remembering the phrase from Olivia.

"Doing our bit for the planet," he agreed.

"I take it that Briony's wedding is going to be a bit more ostentatious."

"Roses, anemones, sweet pea and ranunculus. A lot of white, if you ask me, but the customer is always right."

She smiled in agreement because it was expected. "It was nice that everyone could gather together the other day to remember Cat."

"I think it was something that had to be done," he said, and there was a polite neutrality to his tone that struck Izzy as odd.

"But you were good friends. Or old friends, at least. She came into your shop a lot."

Now his eyes flashed darkly, a sour expression. "Two, three times a week. Never ordered anything. Maybe poked at the wares."

"Yes?"

"She would often start up conversations about what Olivia had done or what she'd heard Olivia had said. She'd show me what things Olivia had liked on social media or screenshots of texts Olivia had sent."

"That's, um..."

"She was stirring, looking for a reaction."

"I thought you and Cat were friends."

He managed a smile but it didn't last. "Friends are people you like, aren't they? But, from the outside, people assume someone is your friend if you're seen in their company a lot."

"I suppose."

"I don't want to..." He stopped and cleared his throat. "Cat's dead now and that's sad, I guess, but ask yourself how many friends she really had?"

Izzy didn't know what to say. Gavin gently turned her around so she was facing towards Irene Wallerton.

"I could see the anger on Dr Upton's face when she came in to see Irene. Cat had power of attorney over her mum's finances, used the sale of her house to financially support that bakery of hers, and how often did she come in to see her mum?"

Izzy abruptly remembered the hen party, when Denise Upton had drunkenly suggested they should all 'bitch about Catriona'. '*The stories I could tell you,*' Denise had said.

"Cat put herself centre stage in everything Olivia and her friends did," said Gavin. "But that was only by sheer force of personality. Or bullying, if you prefer."

"Gosh."

Gavin finished with the arrangement and brushed his hands together to indicate the job had been completed.

"We have a Contact Us form on our website, people wanting a call back or information before making an order. We used to get our fair share of prank messages, asking us to call back numbers that weren't real or turned out to be the numbers for local pizza companies. Childish stuff but it happens."

"Yes?" said Izzy.

"In the last two weeks, since Cat's death, nothing. Not one."

"Wow."

He nodded, his point made. He gestured at her crossed arms. "Nice eggs."

"Thanks," she said and went back to join Nanna Lem. Since Nanna Lem seemed to be very much into her knitting at the moment, it occurred to her that she might ask the woman to knit a present for a friend.

28

Penny had yet to see out a year as co-manager of Cozy Craft, but she thought it was reasonable that trade would be quite slow for much of January. There had been a mini rush in the lead up to Christmas and Izzy had made a small killing with little packs of 'stitch your own Christmas elf' containing sections of fabric and a pattern of her own devising. But now in mid-January, with people counting their pennies after the holiday excesses and waiting for next payday, the shop was pretty much dead.

On Thursday evening, by unspoken agreement, they finished off the little tasks they were doing, put the kettle on, broke out the custard cream biscuits and sat down by the counter to put together everything they knew about Catriona Wallerton's death.

"Cat was not well liked by quite a few people," observed Penny.

"It's more complicated than that, isn't it? It seems Cat was a person who was capable of being a person's best friend and most terrible bully all at the same time. She was entirely unrepentant about the fact that, as a teenager, she got Briony high and caused her to fall off a roof and break her leg."

"She ripped apart the dress you made her for her sixteenth birthday," said Penny.

Izzy paused mid biscuit selection. "Is it ridiculous that that still smarts? More than a decade has passed, and it still hurts."

"Unrepentant," said Penny. "And then there's that stuff, perhaps only rumour, about how she treated her mum and her mum's money."

"I've heard it from more than one source, and Gavin is convinced that Denise knows the details. Cat basically robbed her own mum, shoved her in a home and then completely ignored her. And then there's the stuff Gavin was saying about Cat still clinging to him. The visits to the shop, the prank messages. Maybe she wasn't making anyone's life a living hell, but she certainly was a thorn in a lot of people's sides."

Penny nodded thoughtfully. "So, if we were to take an extreme view on this, we see a woman who has bullied and lied and manipulated her way through life, even bullying her way into being Briony's bridesmaid."

"What's the non-extreme view?"

"Socially incompetent," Penny shrugged. "Some people just don't see what effect their thoughtlessness has on others. Maybe Cat actually thought she was a kind and generous friend to Briony, that her interactions with Gavin were purely playful fun. Cat by name…"

"You think no one ever told her?" said Izzy.

"People can be deaf to what they don't want to hear. Help me out here." Penny took several custard creams out of the packet and placed them on the counter.

"What are we doing?" asked Izzy.

"Imagine each of these biscuits is one of the lodges at Letheringham Hall."

"Ah! Okay!" Izzy moved them around into a loose circle. "We need something to represent the path and the trees."

She went and fetched three spools of decorative braid. Two lengths of green braid became the line of trees. A russet red length served as the path running down from the hall to the lake and through the lodges.

"You'll see here that the fencing by the trees really hems in the lodges at the top," said Izzy. "We checked the other night. Aubrey nearly tripped over a discarded box of chocolates but there was definitely no way through."

"Chocolates?"

"Vegan chocolates. I wondered if Olivia had brought them along that night and left them outside or — anyway. Not the point. Going up to the hall or coming back down from it means you have to go along the path and as soon as you get to sort of here..." She dropped a short pencil across the path. "... then you set off the security lights. I don't care what anyone else says, I had that security light pointing right at me through the flimsy curtains. If anyone had come down in the night, I would have been woken."

"That's a bold assertion," said Penny. "It means that if Cat was killed then her killer was already down there among the lodges."

"And it was possibly one of us," Izzy agreed. She pointed at a custard cream biscuit. "So, this was the biggest lodge, where Briony and Shirley were staying and where we had our drunken hen night. Going round, there was Monica's and then mine and then Denise's and Olivia's and Cat's. Funny thing…"

"Yes?"

"Denise and I had a moment of confusion over which of us was in which lodge, and then she asked me which way was east."

"Right?"

"It took me a while to remember that Olivia had originally complained that she didn't have a veranda facing east."

"Is that a thing people complain about?"

"*And yet*, when I got up the morning after the hen party, there was Olivia on her veranda doing yogic sun salutations or whatever to the cloudy sky." She tapped the pertinent biscuit. "And Denise was right, Olivia *did* have a lodge that faced east."

"So, she's not great at working out compass directions?" Penny hazarded.

The shop door jingled as it opened and Denise Upton entered, closely followed by Aubrey Jones. Monty in his basket barked once in greeting, and sniffed the air.

"You wait for one customer and suddenly two come at once," Izzy declared.

"Sadly, not here to shop," said Denise. "I've got an afternoon clinic to get to."

"And here was me thinking Aubrey was helping carry

your shopping," said Penny, pointing at the bulky carrier bag in Aubrey's hand.

"Oh, we just bumped into each other in the street," said Aubrey. "I've just finished up the work at Sal Butterwick's new shop and thought I'd drop this in to you." He raised the carrier bag. "Stage three in Operation Stop Penny Freezing Her Socks Off."

He presented the carrier bag to her. Inside was a boxy package wrapped in pink floral paper.

"Oh. Oh, thank you," said Penny. "You are being far too generous."

"If I can't help you keep warm on a winter's night, what can I do? Stage four might involve Aubrey's famous three bean spicy casserole."

Denise hoiked a thumb at him. "This man is too nice, right?"

"It's almost as if he wants something," Izzy muttered, amused.

"Anyway," said Denise, "I thought I'd drop by and tell the Famous Five Mystery Gang —" She looked round and counted. "Well, some of them at least. I spoke to my friend on the force."

"We have inside connections now, do we?" said Penny, surprised.

"We do," said Denise. "She spoke to a colleague of a colleague, and it turns out Cat didn't drown."

"She didn't?" said Izzy.

"I said it was really hard to drown in concrete," said Aubrey.

"The coroner hasn't said anything official but it looks like she died from a blow to the head."

"Like she tripped, banged her head and sank," said Penny.

"Or she was hit over the head and then..." Denise pursed her lips as though looking for a better word but not finding one. "... she was disposed of in the concrete."

"Murder," said Penny.

"Pre-meditated murder," said Izzy.

"The police are now investigating properly but I don't think there's much evidence for them to go on. The lodges have all been cleaned out by housekeeping and the hotel doesn't have any CCTV down there. But here's the weird thing..."

"Oh?" said Penny.

"They did take casts or images or whatever of the footprints in the concrete. And they could only find prints of the left shoe."

"That's because I found the right shoe on the bench," Izzy pointed out.

"No, no," said Denise. "I mean, ignoring the fact that no one else saw that shoe apart from you, I mean they only found prints of the left shoe, no right footprints at all, shoe or no shoe!"

Penny frowned. "You mean she *hopped* across the concrete?"

"That's definitely one interpretation. Interesting, huh?"

"That's one word for it," said Aubrey. "We're talking about a person's death, which is just tragic, really."

"Sure," said Denise, who didn't seem particularly

impacted by the tragedy. "But fascinating. Anyway, duty calls."

"Yes," Aubrey agreed. "Have to tidy away at Sal's shop."

He held the door for Denise as they both headed out.

"You'll have to tell me more about this spicy bean casserole," Denise said, and then the door closed on their conversation and the wind.

"Hopping footprints and a head injury," said Izzy. "And Aubrey's bought you another present. It's almost as if he likes you."

Penny didn't reply. She was trying to digest the information Denise had imparted.

"Tell you what," said Izzy. "I'm going to put the kettle on again and then you can open your present."

29

Two fresh mugs of tea were steaming on the counter next to the biscuit-and-fabric reconstruction of the forest lodges.

Penny opened Aubrey's gift with some reluctance. "Same paper as the house coat," she observed, pointing at the floral wrapping paper.

"Detective Izzy suggests that it's been gift wrapped by the same shop, unless he's pinched a load of wrapping paper from some elderly relative."

"You are enjoying this way too much," said Penny.

"Sorry," said Izzy, but she did not look at all sorry. "Nice paper. I might keep it and reuse it."

Penny unwrapped the parcel to reveal a huge tartan boot. Its label showed a picture of a woman sitting with both feet in the boot and smiling enthusiastically.

"It plugs in," said Izzy. "It's an electric foot warmer."

Penny turned it over in her hands. "So when I am sitting

in my chair, I can put my feet in it and they'll get warmed up by the power source."

"Don't forget that the rest of you will be snuggly in your pink house coat," said Izzy. "All you need now is a hat like Wee Willy Winkie and you'll be ready to go into full hibernation." She made a show of searching around in case the hat had been misplaced.

"How old does Aubrey think I am?" whispered Penny. "He's well-meaning, and it's clear he's trying to offer solutions to a very real problem, but in doing so he seems to be treating me like an old lady."

"I bet he's quite the domestic hero," said Izzy. "Everything tidy and put away, all maintenance done promptly."

"A proper homebody," said Penny. She realised as she said it that the idea was somehow stifling. "I'll put this with the housecoat." She dropped the giant heated slipper down by the side of the counter.

"It's the thought that counts," said Izzy.

"I'm not sure what the thought is here, though," said Penny and shook herself to put it from her mind. "So, Cat got clonked on the head and hopped into the concrete."

"Not likely," said Izzy. "It seems there's a clearer explanation."

"Do tell."

"Cat was murdered."

"Yes, I think we're agreed on that."

"And then the murderer used her shoe, the one that hadn't fallen off while Cat was being dragged down to the lake, to make a series of pretend footprints in the concrete. The murderer wants us to think that Cat stepped in and drowned but this recent evidence indicates even more clearly that the scene was staged."

Penny nodded. "That makes sense."

"The murderer went back to find the other shoe but didn't collect it until after I'd noticed it."

"So, there's a hidden shoe somewhere."

"Perhaps."

Penny waved her hand over the scene. "And we are left with six potential murderers."

Izzy's lips moved briefly. "Are you including me in those six?"

"I'm just being thorough. Besides, Cat did rip up a dress you lovingly made with your own hands."

"Half a lifetime ago!"

"I'm just putting it out there," Penny grinned. "Okay. Briony's motive is what? Revenge for breaking her leg when they were teenagers?"

"And for being the worst best friend imaginable. Reading between the lines, Cat forced Briony to take her on as a bridesmaid."

"Shirley's motive would be the same but amplified by a mother's protectiveness. As we have heard Shirley say, Cat ended Briony's chances of a career as a dancer."

"All mums think their children are going to be superstars."

"Did yours?" said Penny.

"Still does," said Izzy. "And she's right. Superstar dressmaker and all round crafter. But yes, Shirley never disguised her dislike for Cat or for the influence she had over Briony. From a purely practical dimension, it would make sense if Shirley and Briony had worked together to kill Cat. They were in the same lodge and lunking a body about would probably require two women."

"Which brings us to Olivia. Olivia would know that Cat was no good for Briony, but worse than that, Cat seemed to cling to some jealous possessiveness over Gavin. Depending on how strongly we want to interpret what you heard from Gavin, it's possible Cat was orchestrating a vindictive campaign against them."

Izzy put a finger on the next biscuit. "Denise has the most understandable motive of them all, in my opinion."

"You reckon?"

"She is Irene Wallerton's GP. She knew how Cat had abused her power of attorney to get the money to fund her shop. And she knew how Cat had abandoned her own mother at the very moment Irene needed her the most."

"True. But Denise has been very helpful in our amateur sleuthing."

"Staying close to the investigation. Pretending to be helpful to avoid suspicion."

"A very cynical perspective, Izzy King."

"Just laying down the options."

Penny looked at the last biscuit. "Monica. She barely knew Cat."

"Cat called her an ugly duckling, well, sort of implied it."

"That's not murder material."

They both looked at the biscuit and pondered.

"Monica is not a fan of this marriage," said Izzy eventually.

"No…"

"We're making Monica a deliberately provocative outfit. And the death of the cake maker and bridesmaid does rather put a crimp in things."

"She wants to stop the marriage going ahead? And that justifies murder?"

"If she's determined to protect her brother from a bad match," said Izzy and then she grunted.

"What?" said Penny.

"Something Nanna Lem said. She was of the opinion that marriages don't have to start out with the couple being in love, that love is something that gets built over time and doesn't magically come from above."

"I don't know if that's sweet or cynically unromantic."

"My thoughts entirely!" Izzy ate a custard cream as she ruminated. "Nanna Lem didn't go so far as to suggest that people who believe in true love or soul mates are nutters but…"

"You've eaten Cat's lodge," said Penny, indicating the half-eaten biscuit Izzy now held.

"Oh, sorry. No, this is Olivia's lodge. It's…" She frowned. "You know what, Cat and Olivia fell out that night because Cat had let Olivia eat some bacon-infused cornbread."

"You mentioned."

"And then they were both outside and when they eventually came back in, apparently the argument had been all patched up."

"Your point?"

"The next day, Olivia definitely had the east-facing lodge. What if Cat had tried to make amends by agreeing to swap lodges with Olivia? It's a small enough sacrifice to make."

"Okay. That explains the confusion. But is it relevant?"

Izzy's eyes sparkled with excited thought.

"We've been wondering how on earth the killer got into Cat's lodge. We've been assuming that Cat opened the door to her killer. We've been puzzling over how one of us hens — who are, for the most part, not the biggest or burliest of people — how one of us could have carted Cat's corpse down to the lake."

"Yes? Yes?" said Penny, wishing Izzy would get to the point.

"What if the killer was in Olivia's lodge all along, and then was still there when Olivia and Cat swapped over? What if that was the plan all along?"

"The plan?"

Izzy nodded. "Olivia and Gavin had good reason to despise Cat. They knew that she was a bully. Gavin knew from what he'd overheard at Millers Field that she had effectively abused and robbed her own mum. All the motives rolled into one."

She stabbed a finger at the spot where the biscuit lodge had been.

"Cousin Olivia and Gavin had plotted to kill her all along. No security light came on because Gavin had been there since earlier in the day, originally in Olivia's lodge which then became Cat's lodge."

"Wow," said Penny.

"I know," said Izzy.

"To be clear, we have absolutely no evidence for this theory and it's crazy conjecture but... it's a good explanation."

Izzy grinned. "All we need to do is subtly find out where

Gavin was that night. If he has no alibi then — bingo-bongo! — we know it's him."

"Is bingo-bongo what we say when we identify a murderer?"

Izzy gave her a haughty look. "It can be. Ooh!"

Izzy was looking out of the window. It was just a few wisps in the air, but it had started to snow.

30

Towards the end of the week, Monica came to the shop for a dress fitting. The whole ensemble was not yet finished, but with just over a week left until the big day, they needed to see how the body suit fitted Monica and make the necessary changes. The snow had continued throughout the night and day, falling consistently and finding purchase on the cold dry ground.

Monica stamped snow off her feet on the mat. She looked a little nervous. Penny hoped that they could steer her back towards excitement with the dress. The flashing blue lights of an ambulance went by as the door swung shut.

"We've been having such a fun time creating your outfit," said Penny. "Today we're going to make sure that the underneath parts fit you well, because they will be doing the behind-the-scenes work and they need to be secure, right?"

Monica nodded.

"But the showy part of the outfit is also under

construction, and your reward for doing the dull stuff is that you get to see what's under that cloth over there."

Izzy stood next to the covered mannequin. She posed like a magician's assistant, wearing a big grin.

"Ooh, that sounds fun," said Monica. "Bring it on."

Penny held up the bodysuit. "Did you buy a fancy bra that you don't mind being partially on show?"

"I did," said Monica. "Cost an arm and a leg, so I need to make sure I do show it off, so I can get my money's worth!"

"Well try this bodysuit on over the top of it and we can see that the base layer is sorted. Then we have a structural panel to try out against you."

Five minutes later, Monica emerged from the bathroom wearing the bodysuit and Penny smiled. "That looks good. Does it feel alright?"

Monica nodded. "It does."

Izzy appeared with the foundation piece she had been working on. The upper part was a large triangle, with some enclosed channels that held flexible steel spirals so it would retain its shape. At the base was a waistband that would support it. She held the triangle against Monica's front, with the pointed end towards her neck.

"Imagine the swan's neck will start here. This piece will go underneath the bodice so that it can be shaped like this without it all flopping into the middle."

Monica peered down at the odd-looking thing. "It's like armour or something."

"It's not going to stop a bullet," said Izzy, "but it will stop a fashion disaster."

Izzy spent a few minutes with the piece, bobbing back and forth to get different perspectives.

"I'm happy this will look right. I have a few adjustments to make at the waist, but that's fine. Do you want to get changed?"

Monica nodded a head at the mannequin. "Can't I see that first?"

"Of course." Izzy resumed her showbiz assistant role and approached the mannequin, gripping the edges of the cloth that covered it. "Are you ready for the reveal?"

Monica nodded, and Izzy whisked away the cloth with a flourish. "Ta da!"

Monica was momentarily stunned, and then gave a small squeak of delight and immediately went over to pat the edges of the tulle. "It's got a life of its own! This is going to be so much fun to wear."

Penny was relieved. She had been worrying that no-nonsense Monica might suddenly take fright when she saw the undeniably ostentatious swan dress. That she was excited by it was a weight off Penny's mind.

"We haven't discussed shoes," said Penny. "Do you know what shoes you'll be wearing, Monica?"

Monica's face fell. "Shoes?"

Penny felt like a monster for bringing it up. Surely Monica hadn't forgotten her feet?

"Normally I wear boots with everything. I guess I just thought this would be the same."

Penny looked at the boots which Monica wore, and then looked across at the partially made swan dress on the mannequin. "Well..."

"It's your look, Monica, there is no reason at all why boots shouldn't be a part of it," said Izzy. "The Bjork dress was a jumping-off point, an inspiration. This is not cosplay."

"Right," said Monica. "Will I get away with boots?"

"You've got the best part of a week to think about it," said Izzy. "Someone here," she added, leaning her head towards Penny, "hasn't even begun to think about what's she's wearing."

Monica smiled, mollified. "Oh. Which reminds me, Ross wanted to know the name of your plus one, Penny. You have got a plus one, haven't you?"

Penny knew her face didn't paint a reassuring picture.

"I am going to make that decision today," she said. "Yes, I am."

"You are?" said Izzy.

"I am," said Penny.

"Lovely," said Monica.

31

As the door to Cozy Craft jangled shut, Izzy turned to Penny.

"So who is it?"

"Who's what?"

"Your plus one."

"I said I'd decide today."

Izzy tutted and rolled her eyes. "Aubrey or Oscar. It's a choice between two."

"And I will make that decision."

"I tell you what," said Izzy, and took her scarf off the side and began to wrap it around her neck, "I'm going to go out and check Gavin's alibi for the night of the murder and then, when I return, you will have made your decision."

"Fine!" said Penny, irritated, and then said, "How are you going to check out his alibi?"

"Very simple. I'm just going to ask him. That's how adults

get things done, Penny. They are direct and they simply ask what they want to know."

"Er, okay."

Izzy put on her coat, considered the white snowy sky and took out her knitted mittens too. She stepped out and, rather than walking straight across to Bellforth's florists, walked the long way round to give herself time to think.

"Gavin, where were you on the night of Friday the fifth of January between the hours of ten pm and seven am?" she practised under her breath. She grunted critically. "Gavin, you know the night Cat got murdered? Where were you? At home? Out?" She grunted again. "Gavin, you murdered Cat, didn't you? Surprised I knew? Cat got your tongue?"

She shook her head at her worsening efforts and decided that, like many things in life, it would be better if she just improvised in the moment.

The marketplace in Framlingham was not a perfect square. Market Hill had a curve to it. Cozy Craft and the Crown Hotel were at the highest point, near the exit from the marketplace that continued up the hill towards Framlingham Castle. Down one side of the marketplace there were a couple of buildings containing shops and the Indian restaurant that turned the square of Market Hill into a massively lopsided U-shape. Bellforth's florists and Wallerton's cake shop were hidden in the much shorter strand of the U-shape, and so it was only as Izzy came round the side of the restaurant that she saw the front of the florist's shop.

The door to the shop was open wide, there was a small crowd gathered there, and, more tellingly, an ambulance was parked outside. One of the women from the cake shop was standing there, neck craning to see better.

"What's happened?" Izzy asked.

"Been an accident," said the man on the other side of her. It was James Coombes from Letheringham Hall.

"Sorry. I didn't see you there," said Izzy. "Accident? Who?"

There was movement inside and a paramedic emerged. The man gave the onlookers something of a contemptuous look and then went to the front of the ambulance and got in. Izzy could see he was making a call on his radio, and there was a slow, mannered air about his movements that, on reflection, Izzy decided did not bode well.

"It's Gavin, I think," said James. "Hey! Olivia!"

He was waving now at Olivia, who was hurrying down the pavement towards the shop, Briony Hart close on her heels. James tried to push his way awkwardly through the little crowd to get to her. He managed to intercept her before she got to the door, and put his hands on her shoulders to halt and comfort her.

Izzy peered through the shop window. The shop itself was dimly lit on this sunless day. Beyond the counter and the bouquets of flowers, the other paramedic crouched in a back room. There were what looked like pieces of pottery scattered on the floor around him.

Slowly, James and Briony led an increasingly tearful Olivia inside. Izzy stood there long enough to try to catch Olivia's eye and offer some empty words of sympathy, but Olivia didn't look up once.

Izzy slowly walked back to her own shop.

Penny was poring over a pile of buttons when Izzy entered.

Izzy slowly stripped off her mittens.

"Does it check out?" asked Penny, without looking up.

"Pardon?" said Izzy, still not sure what to make of what she'd just seen.

"Gavin's alibi. Did you speak to him?"

Izzy took off her coat.

"There's been an accident. At the florist."

"What kind of accident can you have at a florist?" said Penny. "Someone trip on a daffodil?" She looked up and saw Izzy's face, and then all amusement was wiped from her expression. "What happened?"

Izzy told Penny what she'd seen. She was also telling herself. There had been so much to take in so quickly, and yet so little indication of what had actually happened. She wanted to say something about the paramedic's casual manner and the scattering of broken pottery on the floor and how those things told her that something very bad indeed had happened to Gavin.

"We'll just have to wait and see," said Izzy.

Penny made her a cup of hot chocolate, reasoning that a sugary hit was perhaps what she needed to get over the shock. After drinking a second cup and refusing a third, Izzy gestured at the buttons Penny had been organising on the counter.

"Sorting buttons?" Izzy asked. "Have we truly run out of other tasks to do?"

"I am using the buttons as tallies while I think about who I should ask to be my plus one for the wedding," said Penny.

"Every time I think of something positive, I put a button in the Aubrey pile or the Oscar pile."

"Whoa! Talk me through it," said Izzy.

"I don't know if this is the time," said Penny, with a small nod to the window and across to Bellforth's.

"I think we could both do with the distraction and I'm not going to give you any excuses to delay this further." She dragged up a stool. "Show me the tallies, Penny."

"So, both Aubrey and Oscar are generous and kind." She put a button in each pile. "I'm pretty sure both of them care a lot for me." Another button for each pile.

"Both have the requisite number of limbs and eyes," said Izzy, putting another button in each pile.

"Being silly about it already?"

"Come on. You'll never get anywhere if you give them both easy wins so they're always level pegging," said Izzy. "How about I ask you a question and you have to say which one of them wins the point?"

"What?"

"Like if I say to you 'which one is the most handsome?', you're not allowed to say that they both are."

"But they are both handsome!" said Penny, and then laughed. "Handsome. Such an old fashioned word. I think I'd only use that word to describe a horse or something."

"Handsome. Fit. Attractive. Whatever, but you have to decide which one is the *most* handsome, right?"

"It's a bit of a shallow question, isn't it?"

"Yes. And yet it still matters to us, doesn't it? Unless you want to start breaking it down by body parts."

Penny blew out a long, contemplative breath. "I guess

Aubrey has the dark and manly thing, where Oscar is more normal looking, just like a regular person. God, is that a terrible insult?"

"We're being decisive here. Put aside your qualms. So Aubrey is the most handsome?"

"Yes. Fine. Let's say that he is." Penny dropped a button onto the Aubrey pile.

"Well done. You can do this. Let's try another question. Which one is the better conversationalist?"

"Hm, interesting. I can chat easily to both of them, definitely. They are both lovely to talk to. I guess the limiting factor is what experiences they bring to the conversation. Oscar travels and meets more people, so he won't run out of things to say. I'd say Oscar gets the point."

Izzy narrowed her eyes. "You're not just saying that because Aubrey got the last point and you want to be even-handed?"

"No," said Penny, obviously lying. "What do you take me for?"

"Right, let's do another. What about a negative one. Who can be the most annoying?"

"No contest. Aubrey. Absolutely one hundred per cent annoying all month with his well-meaning gifts. I wouldn't normally dream of complaining when someone has been so very kind."

"But..." said Izzy, motioning that she should continue.

"But Aubrey is a homebody and it makes me feel trapped and weirdly old before my time or something. It's like... Hang on."

Penny dashed upstairs.

32

Penny came downstairs with the thick, bulging scrapbook that Oscar had gifted her. Penny guided Izzy through it and shared the pictures Oscar had taken on his recent trip to New York. It was clear Izzy couldn't help but be charmed by the excitement of all the things he'd seen, the fashions he'd encountered.

"Thoughtful gifts," said Penny and put the next button in the Oscar pile.

"Aubrey's gifts were thoughtful."

"They were," said Penny. "But it's like... this town. Aubrey treats this town like it's his whole world. And it's lovely and it's charming and, in all honesty, I feel like I could live the rest of my life here. And Aubrey is absolutely a big part of that. He's part of that big comfy blanket around me. But that doesn't change the fact that when I'm with Oscar, chatting with Oscar, it's like he wants to take me by the hand and lead me on a great adventure into the unknown and that makes me feel…"

Penny struggled to express herself and did a wibble wobble motion with her hands like she was a thing made of jelly.

Izzy gave her a silent look. Penny met her eyes and looked at the buttons on the counter. With a sigh, she swept one pile aside.

"I'm inviting Oscar, aren't I?" she said.

"Sounds like it."

Penny huffed.

"You should go make some phone calls now," said Izzy.

Penny huffed again. "Yes. I should. I'll… I'll take them upstairs."

Penny went upstairs again, seeking out Oscar's number as she climbed the stairs. In her room, she sat on the plush purple armchair and looked out of the window as she made the call.

"Hello!" said Oscar. "We must be psychic. I was just going to call you."

"Oh, were you?" said Penny. "Synchronicity. Have you got a minute?"

"Absolutely."

"Good. Just a quick question. You know I asked if you were free on the twenty-seventh?"

"Er, yes, you did." There was the sound of flicking pages. "And I still am. Got exciting plans for me?"

"I don't know about exciting. Would you care to be my plus-one at a wedding in Fram?"

He hummed musically. "Is this going to be one of those

dull cliched weddings with the Christmas icing wedding dress and the hideous morning suits and everyone being horribly smug about themselves?"

"Quite possibly."

"And will this also be the debut of your swan dress confection?"

"That too."

"I can't think of anything I would rather be doing."

"That's fantastic."

"I had wanted to come down and see you anyway. I have some things I wanted to talk to you about."

"Intriguing. I —"

There was a buzzing from her phone. Another call was coming in. It was Aubrey's number.

"Can I send you the details of the wedding weekend?" she said. "I've got another call that I really must take."

"Sure," said Oscar. "What nights do I need to book a hotel for?"

Penny's eyes automatically went to her own double bed in the corner, the one with the super soft mattress and iron bedframe.

"We'll work that out later," she said. "Gotta go."

She ended the call and connected to Aubrey.

"Aubrey, the very man I need to talk to," she said and took a deep breath.

"Ah, the same," he said. "I needed to check something with you."

"Right. I've not yet had a chance to try out the heated boot things."

"Oh. No. Not that," he said, and she could hear his smile.

"No, you mentioned the date of the twenty-seventh and asked me to keep it free."

"I asked if you had anything on."

"Right. Yes. Well, I do."

"You do?"

"I do have something on. And I just wanted to check that wasn't going to be a problem."

She was wrong-footed for a moment or two, and had to recollect herself before she could speak. "No. That's fine. In fact, that's perfectly fine."

"Good, because if you had plans... for me, I mean."

"No. No. It's all fine. Do your thing."

"Great. Speak later," he said and hung up.

Penny looked at the phone.

"Well, that was easier than I expected," she said.

She went downstairs with a lightness in her step. A decision had been made, a date had been selected. Oscar Connelly would be joining her for Briony and Ross's wedding and... maybe that would be the proper start of something more.

In the shop front, Izzy was waiting for her. Penny was smiling, but there was a sombre look on Izzy's face. Izzy had her phone in her hand.

"Word gets round fast," she said. "That was a text from mum. The accident at the flower shop. Some shelves came down or something like that. Gavin is dead."

33

The snow kept coming through the weekend, and although there were long periods of time when it did not snow at all, the dry frigid conditions meant it did not melt either, and so by Tuesday afternoon there was an immaculate blanket over the whole town.

Izzy walk along cleared pavements around the edge of the market place and through the buildings to Fore Street and the Millers Field sheltered accommodation for the meeting of the Frambeat Gazette editorial team. A huge green enamel pot of tea stood in the centre of the table. Beside it was a plate of biscuits, ginger nuts and pink wafers, half and half.

Annalise the librarian poured Izzy a cup as Izzy struggled out of her hat and scarf.

Izzy was not the last to arrive this time. Tariq hurried in, brushing snow from his thick hair.

"And now we can begin," said Glenmore. "Promptly, for once."

"Good," said Izzy. "I've got a date this evening."

"Something exciting planned?" said Annalise.

Izzy looked to the window and the heavy snow that lay on absolutely everything.

"No question of what we'll be doing," she said.

"Er, take one of each biscuit, please," said Annalise as Tariq reached to snaffle two pink wafers. "It's the first round of our biscuit world cup. Thirty-two biscuits enter the knock out stage. This afternoon it's ginger nuts versus pink wafer. I'm going to write a weekly article so I would like opinions."

"Is this what small town journalism has come to?" said Glenmore sniffily.

"It's an issue that will get people talking," replied Annalise, and Izzy could only silently agree with her.

"I'm sure we have other things to write about."

"Like the murder of Gavin Bellforth," said Tariq.

"Is it a murder?"

"The police have yet to comment. But if it's not then it's a freak accident. The shelving unit falling like that and a big terracotta pot landing on his skull."

"Probably says something for the state of health and safety in the workplace," said Glenmore.

Izzy wasn't sure, but his one good hand seemed to twitch as though tempted to cradle the stump of his missing arm. Glenmore had never spoken about the circumstances in which he'd lost his arm and Izzy had never been brave enough to ask.

"I thought we could actually write about it from the 'cursed wedding' perspective," said Tariq.

"Is the wedding cursed?" asked Annalise.

"Cat Wallerton who died at Letheringham Hall was not only a bridesmaid but was making the wedding cake. Gavin Bellforth was doing the flowers for the wedding and his girlfriend was another of the bridesmaids."

"Makes you wonder if the whole thing will go ahead."

It was going ahead. Izzy knew this. She'd dropped a sympathy card off to Olivia and had spoken to Olivia's mum, her own Aunt Kathleen. The whole family had folded in around Olivia supportively, although there were few words one could say when someone's partner of several years had died so suddenly. Kathleen had said Olivia was going to do her best to be there on the big day, for Briony's sake, but there was no knowing how grief might take her.

"I'm going to the wedding undercover," Tariq said.

"You're what?" exclaimed Izzy.

"Well, not exactly undercover. I contacted the bride's family and asked if they'd like a second free photographer on the day. I said the Frambeat Gazette would love to do a newspaper feature and I would give them copies of any pictures I took."

"But you're secretly going to be investigating the 'cursed' wedding story. These are some of my close friends and family you're talking about."

"Of course," said Tariq, realising. "You know the involved parties. I must quiz you later."

"Nutty," said Glenmore.

"Exactly," said Izzy.

"A little spicy for some people's tastes."

"Pardon?"

"But overall, quite a reliable biscuit."

He was holding up a half-eaten ginger nut biscuit. He realised that both Tariq and Izzy were looking at him.

"I think it's a good idea, actually," he said. "A bit of initiative from young Tariq here. However, I would look upon the matter very dimly if I heard our roving reporter was making a nuisance of himself on the big day."

There was something about the way the old man said 'very dimly' that seemed to put the fear of God in Tariq.

"Photographers should be seen and not heard," added Izzy.

When the meeting was done and the biscuits had been consumed and judged, Izzy stepped away from Millers Field in her thick coat, scarf and hat. She was wearing mittens and she slapped them together with a dull thwack as she walked towards Marcin's farmhouse. Winter darkness and the sharp streetlights seemed to make the snow piled up in the road and gutters glow with its own inner light.

On the walk along Station Road, she saw footprints in the most recent snowfall. Little angled bird feet and little clawed holes that might be dogs or possibly foxes.

At Marcin's, Izzy was buzzed through into the yard and she crept forward, gathering snow as she went. She pressed it into a ball in her mittened hands and, when she caught sight of Marcin coming over from his house, she launched her missile at him. She caught him on the upper arm, but when he turned she saw that he was carrying a snowball that was as big as a football in his bare hands.

"No!" she squealed and ran for cover.

He heaved it with a chuckle but it fell short.

"I went too big too soon," he observed as he scooped up a smaller handful.

Minutes later they had both scored several direct hits and collapsed with laughter at the outrage that each one sparked. A mouthful of snow was an oddly shocking but hilarious thing.

"And now we build a snowman," said Marcin.

"Yep, I hope you know I want a really massive one," said Izzy. "Massive body, massive head and all the trimmings. It should be so huge that it's still here in June."

"Let us do it," said Marcin. Together, they began to roll two snowballs across the ground so they would pick up more snow. When they got too big for one person to move easily, they helped each other to roll the larger of the two.

"This is a good body," said Izzy. "Let's get the head on and then we can pack some more snow on the sides."

They heaved the smaller snowball on top and slapped handfuls of snow all over to increase its bulk.

"We need a carrot and some other stuff to make its face," said Izzy.

Marcin nodded and fished in his pocket. "Carrot and two sprouts for eyes. I don't have any coal, and I think our snowman will appreciate the vegetables."

Izzy put them in place and stood back. "He is magnificent!"

"Some photographs and then we go inside to warm up, yes? My hands are cold."

She looked at his bare hands. "Still not found your glove?"

"I will have to buy some new ones."

"Don't be so hasty," she said.

Marcin and Izzy posed for pictures with their creation, then went inside. They removed their soggy outer garments and went through into Marcin's living room where an open fire was already burning.

"I will add more logs, we will soon be very warm."

Izzy moved their boots and gloves in front of the fire because nothing was nicer than slipping on warm boots.

"Gluhwein?" asked Marcin.

"A warm fire and a glass of gluhwein? Yes, please."

One of Marcin's dogs had claimed the rug in front of the fire. He had some dogs who lived in the house and some others who lived in the outbuildings. Izzy stooped to tickle the happy creature's ears.

"Do you believe in curses?" she asked.

"That is an odd question," he said.

"This wedding…"

"Ah, the dead florist. Yes. No."

"Yes no?"

"Yes, I understand. No, I do not believe in curses. My great grandmother used to tell me a story."

"Is this the great grandmother who was a secret ninja assassin during the Second World War?"

"That is not how she would have described herself but yes. She told me a story of a man who one winter decided to end his own life. This was in the Carpathian Mountains and life was hard in winter."

Izzy wiggled her toes in front of the warming fire. "So hard."

"So, the man picked up his revolver, put one bullet in the chamber, spun it and shot himself in the head. *Click*. The hammer fell on an empty chamber. The next day he did the same. He spun the chamber and pulled the trigger. *Click*. Every day for a week he did the same and still he did not die. The man was good with maths. Polish education is among the best in the world. After four attempts — *click, click, click, click* — he knew that the odds were he should have killed himself by now. After two weeks, still not dead, he calculated there was less than a one in a hundred chance of him having survived that long."

"Lucky."

"Exactly. That is what he thought. Not cursed but the opposite. In fact, he did think he had been blessed by the saints and so after a month of this, he concluded that his life was being spared for a purpose and resolved to do something with it. He went out into the forests to hunt dangerous bears. He met a bear and the bear killed him."

"Oh," said Izzy, who had not been expecting the story to end so abruptly.

Marcin sipped his gluhwein.

"The man thought there was something magical and meaningful about his situation. If he had just stopped to think for a moment he would have realised that his pistol was old and the chamber spindle was very loose and every time he had spun the chamber, the weight of the one bullet had pulled it down to the bottom, away from the hammer and the barrel."

"I see. So, no curses?"

"No. Your wedding —"

"Not my wedding, exactly."

"The wedding. There has been a series of bad mishaps. You can either put it down to chance or work out why these things have happened. People may see links but they often confuse causation and correlation."

"Causation and correlation," said Izzy. "Big words."

"As I say, Polish education is among the best in the world."

Izzy leaned over and put a firm kiss on Marcin's lips. "I like your great grandma's stories."

"I don't usually get kisses when I tell them," said Marcin honestly.

"Don't confuse causation with correlation," said Izzy and kissed him again.

34

By the following morning, Izzy had reached the point where she was ready to assemble the swan dress. The head would be attached to the top of the tulle-covered outer layer, the foundation would be positioned beneath, and then she would add more tulle to cover up the joins where the internal waist stay was fastened to the dress.

"I've been dreaming about tulle," she said to Penny. "I think it was tulle, anyway. Now I come to think of it, after bouncing around on it, I ate it. It tasted like marshmallows."

Penny rolled her eyes. "Your sweet tooth even colours your dreams!"

"Of course," said Izzy. "Are there any of those cat biscuits left?"

"You know very well that there aren't. Maybe I'll go and fetch us some when you've finished the swan dress, as a celebration."

Izzy gave Penny a thumbs-up and a grin, and then got

back to the sewing. Quite a lot of this project required hand sewing, although she planned to machine around the waist stay.

Thirty minutes later the door sounded, but Izzy left Penny to tend to the customer, as she was carefully lining up the swan head with the dress and she needed to concentrate. It wouldn't do to have the swan sitting the wrong way round.

"Ladies, please tell me you can help me!" It was Briony, sounding distressed.

Izzy carefully put down the swan and looked over to see what was the matter. Penny was already there with a hand on Briony's arm. She guided her over to a chair, correctly judging that she was extremely distraught.

"What is it?"

Briony held up a carrier bag and swallowed hard before she was able to speak. "It's my veil."

Penny took the bag and extracted a veil from it. She laid it out on the cutting table.

Izzy peered at it. It was a vintage style, possibly from the sixties. The head piece was covered with white satin and had some small periwinkle flowers peeking out from between gathers. The panels of the veil were edged with ribbon, but the larger of the two had a large and noticeable hole in it.

Izzy tried not to think of this as another wedding curse. "Oh dear. What happened, Briony?"

"I saw a crease in it and I thought it would be all right if I gave it a bit of an iron. I swear the iron was on low, but as soon as it touched the material, it made a hole. I'm such an idiot. It was my grandma's and I've ruined it."

Izzy felt terrible for Briony. Izzy had melted a fair few

things in her time but melting your own bridal veil three days before the wedding was the sort of stress that would reduce any bride to tears.

"You want to know your options?" Izzy said, her mind racing.

"Yes please," said Briony, "I know I could go and find another veil. Mum's convinced that's the only sensible thing to do, but I was so looking forward to wearing this one." She sniffed and began to sob.

Penny passed her a box of tissues and looked to Izzy.

"Right," Izzy raised a hand and counted off on her fingers. She didn't yet know how many fingers' worth of ideas she had. Only time would tell.

"Option one is that we shorten this panel of the veil to cut away the hole. It makes the veil into a different style, but we can re-use everything there." Another finger. "Option two, we patch the hole and disguise the mend with some patterns of sequins or something else that we repeat over the whole panel. Option three is that we replace the whole panel." She glanced over at the remaining tulle and knew in her heart that there wasn't going to be enough to do that. Was there an option four? "Um, option four, we make more holes and turn it into a lace effect. Might be a bit too Halloween though, that one." Izzy was done, and lowered her hand.

"There you go, Briony," said Penny. "Izzy is a genius, thinking of all those options. What are your thoughts?"

Briony looked a little more cheerful. "Yeah, cheers Izzy. Not sure I want a short veil, it's the length that has all the drama, isn't it?"

Penny and Izzy nodded.

"I think the patching idea and the lace idea would work well for someone who can carry off that quirky fun look, but I really love this veil for its wholesome simplicity. Your option three sounds best. Can you replace the panel with a new one?"

Izzy had really hoped that Briony would go for any of the other options. "So we need to take a careful look at timings here. Penny, how long will it take to get another bolt of tulle?"

Penny was on the spot now. She could see what the problem was and she was thinking fast. "It's normally four or five days. I could see if Oscar could bring some over but he's not coming down until the morning of the wedding. That's cutting it too fine."

The door went again. Izzy was monitoring Briony's expression, so it took her a moment to drag her attention away to see who the arrival was.

Monica came in, beaming and extending her legs to show off shiny new boots. "Hey, check these out. Wedding boots!" She paused and saw that everyone looked tense and worried. "What on earth is the matter?"

Izzy indicated the veil on the cutting table. "We're trying to work out how we can get hold of some more tulle to fix Briony's veil."

"Oh no," said Monica. She stepped forward and examined the fabric more closely. "Don't say that my dress has used it all up?"

Izzy gave a small nod.

"But," Monica strode around and pointed at the last

length on the bolt, beside where Izzy had been working. "There's some left still. Isn't there enough there?"

"There's not enough to finish your dress and do the veil," said Izzy.

Briony was paying close attention to the conversation now. Izzy could see that Penny was very uncomfortable. Was it the responsibility of Cozy Craft to have contingency plans in case of damaged veils? Penny would probably say yes.

"Well," said Monica. "I hope you realise that there is only one sensible solution to this. The remaining tool —"

"—tulle."

"Tulle," said Monica in a hokey French accent. "The remaining tulle must go to repair the veil. It's Briony's day."

"But what about your dress?" Penny asked.

"I'll leave it to Izzy to get creative. Shorter skirt, bare patch, skull and cross bones patch, I dunno. There will be an answer, I'm sure."

Izzy blew out her cheeks. There would be an answer. "Leave it with me. We will fix the veil and somehow, we will finish the dress."

After Briony and Monica had left, Izzy stood over the swan dress with Penny at her side.

"What will you do?" asked Penny.

Izzy held it up, letting it drape over the curve of her hand so that she could see all of the layers. "I think I can remove some of the layers from further up and put them down here. It might reduce the volume slightly but it's still going to be an amazing dress."

"In the meantime, I'll get in the order for some more

tulle, in case we get any more bridal emergencies," said Penny.

Izzy picked up the seam ripper with a small sigh. It was one thing to remove seams when she'd made a mistake, but removing seams that were supposed to be there just felt wrong.

35

Penny stood in the doorway of Cozy Craft and watched the snow falling as she waited for Oscar to collect her. The constant snow seemed like a muffler around the world, and everything was silent. Monty had been sent up the road to Sal Butterwick, who had kindly offered to look after him for the day. Penny would have asked Izzy's parents or dog trainer Marcin to dogsit him, but they were all going to be at the wedding of Briony Hart and Ross Blowers.

Oscar's polished saloon car rolled up Market Hill and stopped outside the shop. Penny went out to greet him and he stepped out to meet her.

The dress code for the wedding had been the mysterious 'semiformal', but Oscar had taken that in his stride and wore an immaculate suit fitted perfectly to his body. He took both her hands in his and placed a kiss on her cheek.

"Your carriage awaits."

Penny climbed into the front seat. The heater was turned up to its toasty maximum. She directed him via the one way route through town back round to Station Road and Marcin's farmhouse. Izzy, dressed in a coat dress of rich blue boiled wool, and Marcin, in a suit far more pedestrian than Oscar's, were soon ensconced in the back seat of the car.

"This is very kind of you to give us a lift, Mr Connelly," said Marcin.

"Oscar, please," he said, turning to shake hands.

"Marcin," said Marcin, warmly shaking.

Oscar took the ride to Letheringham slowly. It was a journey of less than five miles, but the roads which had been cleared the day before were already being covered by fresh snow. The definition between road and verge and between verge and fields was increasingly hard to make out. The snow-clogged hedgerows were the best guide as to where the road actually was.

"Do I understand it that this wedding is going to be a subdued affair if two of the key guests have died in the past month?" said Marcin.

"Two?" asked Oscar.

"The florist," said Penny. "Gavin Bellforth, boyfriend to the chief bridesmaid, Olivia."

"Blimey. Unlucky."

"Not unlucky," said Izzy from the backseat.

"You suspect foul play?" said Oscar. In his cultured urban accent, the question sounded arch, almost theatrical.

"Murder," said Izzy.

"Possibly murder," said Penny. "And if it is, then one of the guests at the wedding is the likely culprit."

"Like the woman who commissioned the swan dress?"

"Monica," said Izzy. "She's not a fan of her brother marrying Briony. Although whether that's motive enough to kill the cake maker and the florist isn't clear."

"The bride is a more likely suspect," said Penny.

"The bride getting married?" said Marcin.

"Or her mum. Or the two of them together. Cat Wallerton was a bully to Briony and, whether deliberately or not, Cat and Gavin were responsible for Briony falling off a roof and breaking her leg."

"Years ago, when she was a teenager," Izzy added.

"An angry mother is a dangerous thing," said Marcin.

"Wow, any other murderous souls I should know about?" said Oscar.

"It's possible that our cousin Olivia did it," said Izzy, "even though the second victim was her boyfriend. Cat and Gavin used to be an item. It's possible that Olivia learned they had rekindled that relationship. Although Gavin himself seemed to have a very low opinion of Cat."

"But then there is the business of Cat and Olivia swapping lodges on the night Cat was killed. I'm sure Olivia is part of it somehow," said Penny.

"And then there's Dr Denise Upton," added Izzy.

"Who is lovely, really," Penny pointed out.

"Oh, yes. Really nice. But she knew Cat had been taking advantage of her elderly mother and Gavin knew that Denise knew."

"So," said Marcin slowly, "this is not just a wedding. It is one of those murder mystery dinner events?"

"Do we get to stand up during the dessert course and make our accusations?" said Oscar warily.

"I think we will all be well behaved," said Penny. "This wedding has had enough hiccups without any outbursts from us."

She tried to angle this comment at Izzy but it was hard to make a pointed remark when you were all sitting in the same car.

The trees along the driveway to Letheringham Hall offered some shelter from the snow and soon they were at the front of the hotel building. Marcin looked around the snowy ground and the partially buried topiary.

"This is very Jane Austen," he said.

"Isn't it?" said Izzy gleefully, taking his arm.

The four of them hurried inside and a member of staff directed them to a ballroom where pre-ceremony drinks were being offered. The place was already thronged with something close to a hundred guests.

Penny picked up a glass of champagne from a passing tray and smiled at Oscar. Letheringham Hall was decorated in the most spectacular style, with open fires to make it warm and welcoming. Chairs and sofas that looked like genuine antiques were spaced around in convivial groups and the plush carpet underfoot was in sharp contrast to the thick, chilly blanket of snow outside. Izzy and Marcin huddled over two pieces of paper.

"What's that you're studying?" asked Penny, curious.

"Wedding bingo," said Izzy. "Marcin and I are having a race to get a full house."

Penny looked at their cards. Both contained a grid, although the contents were slightly different.

"I can already tick off champagne served on a silver platter," said Izzy with a smile.

Oscar peered in to take a look. "Are some of these challenges? There's one here that says 'start a conga line'."

"Yes they are. Probably those will come a little later when everyone's more relaxed," said Izzy.

"You mean drunk," teased Penny.

"I probably do, although I can see a few people that could do with relaxing. I think they're anxious because the bridal party isn't here yet. I expect Briony plans to be fashionably late and make a big entrance. Then hopefully everyone can settle in and enjoy the occasion."

"Even Olivia?" Penny asked, looking across the room. Olivia was tidying a table piled with wedding gifts and chatting to Ross Blowers

"I know she wouldn't want to miss this," said Izzy with a wistful smile. "She's such a trooper, I'd imagine she's just trying to keep busy."

"Take her mind off her Gavin for the day," Marcin said.

"With flower arrangements everywhere?" said Oscar doubtfully.

"The groom is here," Penny pointed out, as the thought suddenly struck her. "He's not travelling in with Briony?"

"Ross stayed over at the hotel last night. Briony and Shirley are to arrive here in time for the ceremony. Briony's had her hair and make-up done at home so that Shirley can supervise."

Marcin looked at his watch. "The ceremony's quite soon. Hopefully they're on the way."

Penny saw James the event manager scuttle across the room. He did look concerned, but perhaps that was just the pressure of the big day. He would be very busy making sure that everything went without a hitch.

Movement from another corner caught Penny's attention.

"Why are there two photographers?" she asked. She could see two people, both with large camera bags on their shoulders, jockeying for position as they snapped pictures of the waiter who had just delivered the champagne. They turned to snap a waitress as she emerged with canapes and Penny recognised one of them. "Er, that's Tariq from the paper."

"Yeah," said Izzy. "He wants to make sure that the Frambeat Gazette gets its own exclusive pictures."

"He looks as if he's getting under the feet of the official photographer," said Penny. "Probably quite annoying."

"Welcome to my world," murmured Izzy, toasting the frustrated photographer across the room.

36

Izzy mingled with the other guests in search of two people wearing the same item, which was something she had on her bingo sheet. She fancied her chances, as the range of attire for a winter wedding was more limited. There were lots of dresses in rich jewel tones and luxury fabrics, but she hadn't yet spotted a duplicate. Ross the bridegroom had appeared, and she saw James rush over to him with a look of deep concern. She drifted over to check whether anything was amiss.

"Completely stuck? You're joking!" Ross said.

James shook his head. "It's a vintage vehicle and is not equipped with four wheel drive and suchlike."

"What's wrong?" asked Izzy.

James turned to her. "The bridal party are stuck because of the snow. Shirley's place is out past Cretingham. Briony's dad's borrowed a friend's vintage Jag for the day and it can't get off the drive."

Ross looked to James. "What are we going to do?"

"Snow's playing havoc," said James. "Half the serving staff couldn't make it in today. No idea how we're going to get the dinners out later."

"What are we going to do about my bride?" Ross seethed.

Izzy felt bad for James. Being the event manager at a hotel apparently made everything his problem, and he didn't look as if he had a ready answer for this.

"I can try to arrange a recovery vehicle, but I'm not sure how long that will take," said James.

"Oh!" Izzy pointed to the window. "I think I might have an idea. And as for serving staff, just call us up to collect our dinners, like at school."

She clattered down the steps as Monica pulled into the car park in her Land Rover. Izzy ran over to her.

"Monica!"

Monica wound down the window and Izzy trotted round to the driver's side. The vintage four-by-four all terrain vehicle was tall, and Monica sat high above her.

"The bridal party are stranded," said Izzy.

"Like in a snowdrift?"

"Like stranded still at home. We need to go and get them in something that won't get stuck in the snow."

"Well lucky for us, we've got a Land Rover," said Monica, patting the door with affection.

"Exactly my thoughts."

"Hop in and we'll get straight into search and rescue mode."

Izzy climbed into the passenger side, which seemed quite

a long way up. "Well we won't have to do too much searching, as they're still at home. You know where they live?"

Monica nodded. "It's a converted barn at Cretingham. No problem." She glanced at Izzy. "Where's your coat?"

"Forgot to grab it, I was in a hurry."

Izzy's outfit might have been a coat dress but right now, in this snow-blowing breeze, it felt more like a dress than a coat.

"But you remembered your handbag?" she said, noting the bag in Izzy's hand.

"It's got a special something in it for Marcin. I don't want to lose it."

Monica tutted. "There should be a blanket in the back if you can reach it," she said. "Open the heat vent if you want."

Izzy found the blanket, then looked for and located the little hinged door in the dashboard. She opened it and warm air came out. "This is like an actual antique you can drive. I love it."

"She's a beauty, isn't she?" Monica beamed proudly. "Built in sixty-six."

Izzy noticed that Monica was wrapped up in a long green parka. "Are you wearing the swan dress underneath that?" asked Izzy.

"I sure am. It's pretty comfy once it's on. I might need a moment to fluff it up once I get inside. It was a bit tricky to zip myself in, I had to roll on the floor to squash it down enough."

Izzy glanced across to see if she was joking, but apparently she wasn't. This was possibly a first among the clients for whom she had made occasion wear. "Are you going to explode out of there like an airbag when you unzip your parka?" she asked. "You'll need to make sure everyone stands well back."

37

Penny was really enjoying Oscar's company. He had been an excellent choice as her plus-one. He kept the conversation light and entertaining, making jokes with Marcin about what Izzy might be up to after they saw her go running outside.

"I would suggest that her bingo sheet has a challenge where she has to hijack a vehicle and bring a stranger to the wedding," said Oscar. "Am I getting warm?"

Penny heard her phone chime at the same moment as Marcin's, and it turned out to be an explanation from Izzy.

Gone to get the bridal party in Monica's Land Rover, back soon.

"Well she probably doesn't have this on her bingo card," said Penny, holding it up so Oscar could see.

There was another chime, and Penny wasn't quite quick enough to remove the phone from Oscar's eyeline before the next message was displayed on the screen.

You snogged Oscar yet?

"Oh dear. Sorry," said Penny. She could feel herself blushing deep red, right the way down to the deep neckline of her purple velvet dress. She probably looked like a pickled cabbage about now.

"Don't apologise for Izzy, I share her enthusiasm for the subject of, um, kissing," said Oscar, which made Penny blush again. As she looked away, trying to compose herself, she looked over towards the door, where Denise Upton had just entered. There was a tall, suited man with her, and as Penny craned her neck to see who it was, the tall man turned and her eyes locked with those of Aubrey Jones.

Denise had brought Aubrey. Penny felt the blood drain from her face as she registered the surprise of it. Aubrey's gaze went back and forth between Penny and Oscar for a moment, then, with a funny formal smile for Penny, he turned fully to Denise.

Penny texted Izzy.

Aubrey is here as Denise's plus one!

Izzy's reply was swift and unhelpful.

That's nice.

Penny huffed. Denise was a nice person and quite possibly not a murderer, and Aubrey was a nice person, and Penny had picked Oscar, and Aubrey had checked if Penny still wanted him to save the date for her and she hadn't. Everything was somehow fine, so why did she feel so wrongfooted by this development?

Penny pushed her phone into her bag and tried to compose herself as Denise and Aubrey came over.

"Hello everybody," said Denise. "Most of you know

Aubrey, I think."

"So nice to see that the two of you have teamed up," said Penny.

Teamed up? *Teamed up?* Did that make her sound like a good sport, or a weirdo? The look on Aubrey's face suggested weirdo.

"It's nice to have been invited to such a lovely wedding," said Aubrey and it was possible Penny was imagining it, but was there a hidden meaning buried in that sentence, suggesting it was nice to be invited by *someone* to the wedding? Oscar had apparently picked up on something being amiss, as he had a quizzical look on his face. Penny pressed on and introduced everyone.

"Have you met Marcin?" said Penny. "Marcin, Denise. Denise, Marcin. Marcin, Aubrey. Aubrey, Marcin. Denise, Oscar. Oscar, Denise. I'm Penny."

"You're missing Izzy, where is she?" asked Denise.

Aubrey gave a knowing nod. "It'll be a hare-brained scheme."

Penny had to give him that. "You could call it that. She's gone with Monica to pick up the bridal party. They got stuck in the snow."

"Ooh, a drama!" said Denise. She looked around at everyone's faces. "You know how these things are! It might seem like a terrible disaster now, but it will be the tale that they tell for years to come. I'm sure it'll work out fine."

Penny smiled. Denise was wise, too. Of course she was. Still, everyone was checking their watches and wondering when the bride would arrive. This wedding had already experienced more than its share of disasters.

38

Monica turned off the snow covered Friday Street and onto the equally snow covered Brandeston Road that led straight into the village of Cretingham. The Land Rover's wipers struggled to keep up with the driving snow, but at least the powerful vehicle could ride with ease over the ever-increasing drifts.

"I think we're here," said Izzy and pointed beyond the nearest hedge.

Monica's powerful arms turned the wheel and they drove down a short driveway.

Shirley was at the open front door. She wafted a hand in distaste, perhaps at the diesel fumes.

Izzy scrambled down, using the little metal step at the side, so that she didn't faceplant in the snow.

"James assured me that we would be taken care of," said Shirley. "I wasn't expecting this though, I must admit."

It was hard to tell whether the comment was one of gratitude or dismay.

"Mum, is our lift here?" Briony appeared at the doorway in her bridal gown. But for her exposed shoulders and décolletage, she blended perfectly with the local blizzard. "Monica!" she called. "You are such a star, this beast will get through the snow, I bet."

"Well, it got us here, so all it's got to do now is get us all back," said Monica, climbing down. "Now, have you got a big crate or something?"

"I'm sorry?" Shirley didn't look sorry.

"You'll need something to help you step up into the back. Something like a milk crate would do it."

"Do we look as if we've been delivering milk?" Shirley said, wafting a hand at the high heels and stockinged legs that peeked out from her long puffer coat.

"Mum, Monica's trying to help. Let's be practical," said Briony, giving her mother a nudge. "Why don't we get the kitchen stool?"

"Very well," said Shirley. "Someone fetch the kitchen stool."

Briony and Shirley stood staring at each other and then turned their gazes onto Monica and Izzy. There was a heavy unspoken hint that manual tasks were not an option for the bride or the mother of the bride on the day of the wedding.

"Coming through," announced a small balding man in a morning suit.

Briony's dad had brought a stool with fold-down steps. He wiggled the legs in the snow so that it was firmly on the ground.

"Hello, Mr Hart," said Izzy. She couldn't remember the man's name, even though she had met him many times when she and Briony had been teenage friends. He had been a quiet presence, the man of the house, the bread winner, but always a shadowy background figure.

"May I suggest that you will need some blankets as well if you want to be nice and warm in the back there?" said Izzy.

Eventually, with some warm blankets under her arm, Shirley tiptoed carefully through the snow in her expensive looking shoes. She poked a head into the rear of the Land Rover, taking in the bench seats at either side. "Oh my goodness, it's quite primitive in here, isn't it? Are there any seatbelts in the back?"

"No," said Monica. "Built without them."

"Think of it as being like a limo," said Izzy. She wished she'd thought of bringing some of the champagne from the venue, which would perhaps have kept them quiet back there, but they would be at Letheringham Hall soon enough.

Izzy and Monica held out hands to support Briony, Shirley and Briony's father as they climbed up into the rear of the Land Rover and took their seats. They shared the blankets between them and settled in.

"Ooh, this is quite nice," said Briony's dad.

"Yes Dad, it's like a limo but less fancy."

"Hm, less fancy. You're right about that," was Shirley's verdict.

Izzy put the stool in with them and Monica slammed the door shut.

Monica pulled away down the drive and there were squeals from the back as the passengers got used to the deep rocking of the aged vehicle. They drove steadily along the roads back towards Letheringham Hall. Izzy noticed that the tracks they had made just a short while earlier were already completely covered with fresh snow.

"Oh, dear. This isn't good," said Monica, pointing at the road up ahead.

39

Penny peeled away from the group that now contained both Oscar and Aubrey. Was she the only one who was finding things incredibly awkward?

She had faked a toilet trip just to get a breather. She dawdled around the reception of Letheringham Hall trying to collect her thoughts. Oscar was still her date, and he would be fine. In fact, he was currently having a robust discussion with Marcin about fashionable doggy coats. Marcin clearly thought such things were frivolous, but Oscar had put forward the suggestion that they might form an extra channel for Marcin's dog-based business. Penny's thoughts turned to Denise. Penny sighed.

Denise was lovely, and she couldn't imagine a nicer person for Aubrey. It was Aubrey himself that was the problem here, and yet why was that? She had made her choice of who to bring as her plus one and it wasn't him. This was all on her.

"Where did Izzy go?"

Penny was so startled that she jumped. She'd thought that she was alone in the corridor, but James the event manager had appeared. He seemed to have that service worker's absolute gift for moving around silently and unseen.

"Sorry?" said Penny.

"Izzy? She rushed off with no explanation but said that she would sort things out. What am I supposed to do with the timings for the event?"

"She's fetching the bridal party with Monica. You know Monica has a Land Rover?"

"Chef is on my back about his souffles," said James, "and the registrar has another event in two hours."

"She the woman who looks like she should be singing opera?"

"I know what you mean. And yes. But do you have any idea when they will be here?"

"No, not really," said Penny. "Probably not long."

He went to a little nook that was part of the receptionist's area and gazed at a bank of CCTV screens. Most of them looked like there was static interference but, of course, that was just the snow. He pointed at one on the top row.

"The gate entrance. No sign of them."

"Soon. They'll be here soon."

He reached forward and flipped a number of switches. On the screen, two rustic lampposts came on in the grey daylight.

"Think a little beacon will get them here faster?" said Penny, not unkindly.

"I don't know what else to do."

"I mean it should be a straightforward journey," said Penny, although she really wasn't sure.

40

Ahead, Izzy could see that there was an incline which had obviously proven too great a challenge for some vehicles in the snow. Several tracks looped right round where drivers had given up and returned back down the hill. What was more of a problem was that some time after Monica had come down this hill, a climbing articulated lorry had slid into a jack-knife position and blocked the entire road. The driver of the lorry dropped down from the cab and walked towards them, hand gripping the sides of his flat cap to shield his face from the snow. He approached the driver's side and Monica wound down the window.

"Snow! Snow!" declared Shirley irritably from the back seat.

"Are you able to move your lorry?" Monica shouted.

The man shook his head. "Gonna need some help to move it into a drivable position. Nothing I can do as it is."

Monica nodded. "Well, you best hop in the back and come with us. We're off to Letheringham Hall. Just a mile up the road."

"I'm going to Felixstowe," the man argued.

"Not today, you're not. We can take you somewhere warm where you can call for help. I have some friends with winches in their Landies who could probably sort you out."

"Yeah? Thanks." He walked around to the back and gave a small "oh!" of exclamation when he met the three people already in the back. There was the sound of the stool being pushed aside and the door slammed shut before they all shuffled up to make room.

"Off to a wedding, are ye?" said the driver.

"Evidently," said Shirley.

"I'm sure it's good luck to have a lorry driver at your wedding," said Mr Hart.

"That's chimney sweeps, you fool."

"Tyrone," said the lorry driver, touching the peak of his flat cap. "Nice to meet you all."

"This is all very well and good, Monica," said Izzy, "but we can't get past to get to Letheringham Hall. I don't think there's another way around."

Monica gave her a long look. "When you're in a Land Rover there is *always* another way around." She called into the back. "Hold on tight everybody, it's going to get a bit bumpy!"

She steered off the road and onto the verge. Izzy could see a fence about ten feet away, but she had a strong suspicion that there was a ditch between their current position and the fence, and of course it was hidden by the deep snow.

"Hey Monica, do you think there might be a di—" Her words were lost as the Land Rover lurched deeply down and to the side and everyone screamed. Izzy and Monica were belted in, but it sounded as though the passengers in the back were all falling on top of each other.

"It's all right!" shouted Monica. "Worst case scenario, we tip right over and I have to right us with the high lift jack. Nothing I haven't done before."

Once again, Izzy glanced over to see if Monica was joking, but her face was set in serious concentration as she drove along, half in the ditch, and then steered up again and finally righted the Land Rover onto something like a level surface. With a few more bumps they were back on the road again, with the stranded lorry behind them.

Izzy cheered and the passengers in the back joined in.

"Well done, Monica!"

"People should really take more care in snowy conditions," Shirley grumbled.

Mr Hart chuckled. "I recall that you and I only met because you ran your car into the back of mine on an icy road."

"Is that right?" said Briony.

Shirley sniffed. "Your father thinks I did it accidentally. How else was I going to strike up a conversation with him?"

"Took the bumper right off my Ford Fiesta XR2," said Mr Hart. "Gave me a hefty garage bill rather than a regular 'hello' like a normal person."

"Sounds very romantic," offered Tyrone the lorry driver.

The rest of the way up the hill to Letheringham Hall should have been straightforward, but when they reached the entrance, the gate that should have swung open automatically refused to move.

"I'll go," said Izzy, jumping down to press the buzzer.

"Hello," came a tinny voice from the intercom.

"Can you open the gate please?" Izzy shouted.

"It's open," said the voice.

"No, it's really not," said Izzy.

"Let me check the cameras. Oh. Foo!"

Izzy could detect a faint electrical whining sound, which she tracked to the hinges of the gate. "It's making a noise," she said. "I think your gate opening thing is broken or frozen or something."

"Ah yes, this happened once before," came the voice. "Was it the Beast from the East or Storm Emma? The engineer said that it was unprecedented."

"Erm, I have no idea. Do you have any practical suggestions for us to get through to the hall while you're reminiscing?"

"Storm Gillian, I think. Yes. You could walk perhaps? The pedestrian entrance is back down the road by the ford."

"Thank you," said Izzy automatically. Why was she was thanking him for such terrible advice?

She climbed back into the Land Rover. "Gate is stuck. There is a pedestrian entrance somewhere back the way we came. Shall we go and have a look?"

"Did I just hear the words pedestrian entrance?" shrilled Shirley from the back. "You know that the hall is a good half a mile away and we're experiencing a blizzard?"

Monica reversed slowly up the drive without responding, and both she and Izzy peered around, looking for the pedestrian entrance among the trees that surrounded them.

"He said it was by a ford," said Izzy.

They reversed past a turning to the right, marked with a sign.

Not suitable for vehicular access.

Monica glanced at Izzy. "Let's have a look, shall we?"

The Land Rover bounced up the wide path. The snow was deep here, forming a solid blanket between the trees, so there was no way of knowing what the road surface was like, but the bumps and the groans from the passengers in the back suggested that it was very uneven. The road headed down towards what was undoubtedly a ford. Water flowed in front of them in a dark torrent.

Monica put the brakes on.

"Oh look, there's the path!" Izzy pointed at a footpath marked with a yellow arrow. A stile led over the fence and away over to the left, into a field that looked deep with snow. The thought of telling Briony and Shirley that they needed to walk across there in their satin shoes was laughable.

"Hm. Does it look to you as if this track curves left after the ford? It goes in the right direction." said Monica.

"Well yes, I think it does," said Izzy. "Wait, are you seriously thinking about trying to drive through? We don't know how deep it is."

"It's a ford," said Monica. "A crossing point. It should be a bit shallower than elsewhere." She put the Land Rover into gear and inched forward. "We have good high clearance. The trick with these is to maintain a slow but steady speed and just keep going. We might get dragged around a bit, but this is a Land Rover after all."

Izzy enjoyed an adventure as much as the next person. No, that wasn't true. Izzy enjoyed them much more than the next person, but this one looked as if it might be genuinely dangerous. They were moving forward into fast moving flood water in appalling weather conditions.

Monica drove into the ford. It was about twelve feet wide, and as they descended, it became clear that it was also quite deep. Monica followed her own advice and kept going. "Hang on everyone."

They slewed violently to the side as the current tugged at them and everyone cried out, but soon enough they were climbing the other side and bumping up onto the flat surface.

"Any illusions that this is like a limo ride have been thoroughly shattered," said Shirley. "More like the log flume at Alton Towers."

"I, for one, am having the best time," said Tyrone cheerfully.

"There we are, done!" said Monica. "Now, let's find our way to the hall."

Izzy had her phone out, consulting the map function. "It's that way," she said, pointing ahead and to the left. "The map doesn't show fences and things, mind."

The track that they were on was much harder to see once they had emerged from the trees. Monica steered in the direction that Izzy indicated. They climbed an incline, and as they crested it, they could see the roof of the hall. Izzy gave a small whoop.

"Any obstacles you can see?" asked Monica.

"Well, we know there's a lake," Izzy reminded her.

"Goodness yes, of course. Let's avoid that," said Monica. "I reckon if I go straight like this then we'll be grand."

It was a solid blanket of snow, with a few unidentifiable bumps. Izzy couldn't remember what was underneath, but it looked navigable.

Monica picked up a little more speed now she was on the home straight and they drew nearer to the hall.

There was a violent *donk* sound that made Monica brake. "Did we hit something?" she asked.

"A statue," came the shout from the back. "We knocked a statue over."

Izzy suddenly remembered what had been here before. It was a rose garden with statues and benches.

"Oh, I think there might be another one on the other side. Steer slightly over that way and perhaps we'll avoid hitting that one too."

Monica did as instructed and few minutes later they could hear the crunch of gravel under the wheels.

"What about that? We're back on the actual drive!" said Monica. "Hopefully they'll never notice where we've been."

Izzy privately suspected they might have squashed quite a number of rose bushes, but only time would tell.

They drove round to the front, and when they pulled up outside the door, Izzy put the stool in place for the passengers in the back.

They all teetered down onto the ground and looked very grateful to be on terra firma after their eventful drive. The lorry driver emerged last and gazed up the steps at the small crowd, including James and Olivia, who were waiting anxiously.

"Oh blimey, it looks as if there's a wedding on today!" said the lorry driver.

Briony gave him a nudge. "I'm the bride, silly. Come in and join us. It's the least we can do after I ended up on your lap so many times."

41

Penny stood at the window, watching everyone pile out of the Land Rover. There was a man in overalls with them who she didn't recognise and who looked a little confused to be there, but James whisked them all inside.

"Hey, it looks like I was right about Izzy bringing a stranger to the wedding," observed Oscar, giving her a light nudge. "I bet it's on her bingo card."

Penny watched Monica and Izzy put away the stool in the back of the Land Rover and high-five each other as they locked the doors.

There was a delay of a few moments. Penny assumed that Briony and Shirley were removing their coats and straightening their outfits. James walked into the room and held the door open, and everyone turned to watch them enter. Tariq and the wedding photographer each tried to inch closer to outdo the other.

Briony's outfit was an understated white dress in a beautiful, heavy duchesse satin. It was off the shoulder with a wide feature collar and hung in graceful swirls from the waist. It fitted beautifully, and Penny smiled to see her looking so wonderful. The veil sat pushed back on top of her hair, which had miraculously escaped harm from the weather. Penny was delighted to see that the veil had turned out picture perfect, floating backwards in a delicate froth.

Shirley followed behind in an icy blue brocade shift dress, with a long frock coat to match. She looked at Briony with pride, and dabbed her eyes with a white lace handkerchief.

Briony's father wore a smart morning suit with a gorgeous buttonhole, but he was one of those people who looked so uncomfortable in fancy clothes that the overall effect couldn't help being slightly unkempt. He kept a couple of steps behind Shirley and smiled awkwardly at anyone who caught his eye.

The two photographers both dived in and out to capture the outfits and the expressions of the onlookers from different angles. Ross was not present, perhaps hoping to enjoy a surprise all of his own once the ceremony started.

Briony and her parents moved into the room and gratefully accepted flutes of champagne. The hush that had descended as they entered now passed, and there was much excited chatter as they relayed the tale of their journey to everyone.

A few moments later Izzy, Monica and the man who had climbed out of the Land Rover entered the room. Izzy rushed over to Penny. Monica was on her phone, and stood talking. She hadn't even removed her parka.

"We did it! We got them here. Well, Monica did," said Izzy.

"Who's her friend?" asked Penny.

"Tyrone Bambury," said the man, looking about the place with interest. "I can think of worse places to shelter from the weather."

"His lorry is stuck in the snow," said Izzy. "Monica's trying to get some of her Land Rover buddies to help him. We went off-road and it was like being on a roller coaster. You should have been there."

Penny indicated Monica, who was talking on her phone and gesticulating. "She's still got her coat on."

"Well yeah, she's trying to give them directions to — oh, wow. Yeah."

They both turned to look as Monica ended the call and, with a satisfied sigh, put her phone on a side table and unzipped her parka.

"Oh crikey. I said it would be like an airbag going off," said Izzy quietly.

As Monica carefully slid the zip down, the compressed tulle of the swan dress popped out of the gap. It took her a few seconds to completely undo the zip and by that time, she had the attention of everyone in the room as they watched her dress emerge from its khaki chrysalis. She dropped her parka and used both hands to fluff up the tulle of the skirt. It brought a smile to her face as it bounced in her hands. Only then did she realise that everyone was staring.

"Oh hi! Can anyone tell me where I should hang my parka?"

James, the event manager materialised and took her parka. He shook it out and disappeared with it. Penny and Izzy both gravitated towards Monica. Penny thought that perhaps they both felt the same protective urge to support her, as the mood of the room was brittle, almost hostile to the eye-catching outfit.

"You look amazing, Monica!" said Penny. "Seriously, the Doc Martens look fantastic with the dress."

"I enjoyed the exploding tulle show," added Izzy with a smile.

Shirley elbowed her way between Penny and Izzy, cutting them off. "What do you think you're doing, Monica? Seriously, what?"

Monica was unfazed by Shirley's anger. She pointed at herself. "I'm the ugly duckling, remember?"

"The what?"

"Did you not expect me to become a beautiful swan?"

Shirley spluttered with outrage. "You need to get changed out of that right now, young lady, do you hear? White dress to someone else's wedding? Entirely inappropriate! Let me call my friend, Carmella. I'm sure she can find something much more suitable."

Monica continued as if Shirley hadn't spoken. "Let me talk you through Monica's outfit today, because she has put some thought into it, based on your previous feedback." Monica strutted on the spot, making her way along an invisible catwalk. "This outfit addresses some of the key themes in Monica's life. She doesn't always project her individuality and she also doesn't often show off her amazing legs, but this was a rare opportunity to do just that. Most importantly of all, she wants to show that she can look incredible and even a bit feminine if she wants to. Penny and Izzy have helped me realise this dream, and I am delighted to share it with you and Briony."

"Monica, that outfit is amazing!" said Briony.

Shirley was momentarily speechless.

"I am seriously thrilled that my future sister-in-law made such an effort for my big day," said Briony.

Tariq was muttering a voiceover of his own as he circled with his camera. Was he recording voice memos? "Has the head of a swan coiled around her neck. It looks menacing, weird and magnificent all at the same time. It's staring at me right now with its cold dead eyes. Dress is over some sort of bodysuit coloured like flesh, with small diamante stones that catch the light."

Shirley inhaled deeply and slowly, as if by continuing to draw air into her lungs and rise up through the crown of her head she could delay the moment when she needed to speak again. When she did speak again, it was a single word. "Good." She turned on her heel and headed over to James, as if she had urgently remembered that there was a wedding ceremony to attend to.

"Oh hey," asked Marcin as he wandered over, studying his bingo sheet. "Does that count as a socially awkward moment?"

42

The wedding ceremony took place in the orangery. If the hotel's reception rooms were everything that was cosy and warm about an English country house, then this room represented the magnificent and palatial style that could only be achieved in a room with outrageously high ceilings and the sort of architectural detail that had been common in previous centuries. Penny had learned a thing or two about fancy moulded plasterwork when she'd had some replaced in the shop, but the cornices and covings and architraves and in this room were so ornate it was extraordinary. The solid walls had panels that were sculpted and gilded, so that it felt like being in an inside-out wedding cake. Pale gold and ivory were used throughout, with small accents of duck egg blue in the stripes of the wallpaper, which was only featured inside the individual panels. The glass of the roof and the exterior walls were festooned with gauzy drapes that allowed enough wintry sunlight to cheer the room without dazzling its occupants.

The registrar did indeed look ready to sing opera. She was statuesque, and while she was dressed in an understated dress of plum coloured satin accessorised with a peacock brooch, she commanded attention with her upright bearing and her immaculate makeup. She held her arms behind her back and smiled at everyone as she waited to commence the ceremony.

The flower arrangements gave Penny a small pang of regret as she thought of Gavin. She wondered who had stepped in to complete the work, as they looked magnificent. There were two large arrangements at the front and smaller ones arrayed down the sides of the seating area. They incorporated the colours of the room but definitely didn't fade into the background.

She glanced across at Tariq, who had sidled up to Monica a couple of rows in front. She could just about hear their conversation.

"So the swan's eye is essentially a hidden camera? I thought it was looking at me funny when you first arrived!"

"My phone wasn't even in there when I first got here, so I think that might have been your imagination, Tariq."

"You could be taking video of the whole ceremony right now! Imagine how brilliant that would be?"

"Oh yeah. Why didn't I think of that?" said Monica, with a theatrical wink.

Tariq's face was stricken as he realised what this implied. "What? No. Seriously? Oh no. Listen, when I said that stuff earlier about who might catch the bride's bouquet, I was joking, so you can just delete that, yeah?"

Ross stood at the front awaiting his bride. His awed expression when she walked up the aisle on her father's arm caused Penny's eyes to well up slightly. Briony's veil was over her face, and she looked like a soft focus dream as she walked towards Ross with everyone's admiring gaze on her.

She lifted the veil and Ross looked ready to burst with happiness.

"Morning suits and meringue dresses," Oscar muttered lightly.

"Oh, but it's lovely," said Penny.

The ceremony was soon over, and everyone waited in the rows of seats for the bride and groom to lead the way out.

"Nice service," said Oscar. "Sweet, respectful and above all, brief."

Penny nudged him in the ribs. Izzy and Marcin had both judged that they could pull out their bingo sheets at this point, and were busy whispering progress updates to each other.

"The word 'love'. That was an easy one," said Marcin.

"Yep, same. I got 'happiness'," said Izzy.

"I also crossed off 'something blue' because I saw that the wallpaper has a blue stripe," said Marcin, pointing.

"That's not right, 'something blue' is supposed to be something the bride's wearing!" protested Izzy.

"That's not what it says on the sheet, I am taking the point," said Marcin, marking his sheet with a flourish.

"Taken entirely out of context," said Izzy.

Photographs were taken indoors, to avoid everyone

having to go outside in the snow. There were several gorgeous backdrops available in the hall to ensure the pictures were memorable.

Shirley had a stern word with Tariq when he started trying to organise people for his own photographs. She made it clear that the formal pictures were to be orchestrated by the photographer she had hired. Tariq had to make do with taking pictures from creative angles, although Penny could see people becoming increasingly irritated with him peering up at them from their feet. Surely that would never result in a flattering picture?

The star of several of the photographs was the lorry driver who nobody knew. He was being treated as if he were the official lucky charm of the wedding, and everybody wanted their picture taken with him smiling beside them, wearing his delivery overalls.

"It's nice," said Marcin. "The ordinary guy, the worker. He never gets noticed."

Izzy pulled herself closer to Marcin. "I notice you."

"Oh, I am the ordinary guy, am I?" he said.

"In fact, I've got a little something for you somewhere." She made a playful face at him.

"Oh, that reminds me," said Oscar to Penny. "I didn't get to mention the thing I wanted to talk to you about."

"Yes?" said Penny but, at that moment, a man banged a little gong and declared it was time for the guests to go through for their dinner.

43

The orangery had been transformed in quick order into a dining space suitable for a hundred guests. The happy newlyweds, together with both sets of parents plus the beardy best man and chief bridesmaid Olivia, were arrayed along the top table, and ten circular dining tables were set around.

Penny looked to the seating plan on the board as they entered. Their table was not as full as the others, and there were only six names there. She held back any comments when she read those names, and walked stiffly with Oscar over to the table. Izzy and Marcin sat together, Marcin already opening a bottle of wine on the table. Further round from them sat Aubrey and Denise.

Penny honestly didn't know what to do. Life shouldn't be this complicated. She had never been properly romantically involved with him. He'd been a warm friendly presence ever since she'd come back to Framlingham, and he had always been on hand as a source of help, comfort and advice, but they'd never been an item. Yes, there had been drinks and meals together and one memorable wind-tossed night in a shared bedroom in Walberswick when *absolutely nothing* had happened. And yet there had been unspoken moments, and surely he must have realised that her mention of today's date had been a prelude to her potentially inviting him to this wedding. What must he think of her and this new man, Oscar?

It was painfully awkward, and in that massive spectrum, that sea of responses, in which she could ignore him, pretend nothing was amiss or be utterly honest, she didn't know what to do.

She sat down.

"This is lovely!" she declared loudly, and grinned widely. She felt like a bad actor in a school play.

"This is indeed lovely!" said Aubrey in a voice equally false and forced.

"I too think this is lovely," said Marcin honestly, pouring Izzy a glass of white.

Oscar, bemused, said, "Are we all commenting on the loveliness of this situation?"

"Yes," said Denise, equally bemused. "Clearly, we must all say how lovely this is."

Izzy, the only table member yet to speak, looked at them all. "Now, I am feeling peer-pressured to... to use the 'L' word too."

"Never submit to peer-pressure," said Marcin.

"Unless it's fun," said Denise. "Drink?"

Bottles of red were opened to join the white already doing the rounds and Penny gladly took a glass.

Tyrone, the lorry driver Izzy had brought with her to the wedding, came over with a shallow dish of prawn cocktail in his hand.

"Is there room for me to sit here?" he asked.

"Plenty of room," said Penny, who had a grim suspicion as to why this particular table had so much space.

Aubrey pointed a finger at the prawn cocktail. "How did you...?"

Tyrone jerked his head to the side. "They're inviting people up, table by table. Seems they're low on staff today cos of the snow. This chair feels wonky."

"But how did *you*...?"

The man grinned. "I just presented myself at the front of the queue." He tugged at his polo shirt. "I look like a worker, not a guest. If you look like you belong, people just sort of don't notice you," he said and tucked in.

Soon enough, their table was called, and they went up to collect their starters from the short-handed waiting staff. Penny returned and went to sit down again. Denise, Aubrey and Oscar were already seated. There was a wrapped package that had not been there before on the table in front of her seat. The pink floral wrapping paper was *very* familiar.

She looked at it. She looked at Aubrey. He looked at her and smiled.

"Really?" she said.

"Really?" he said.

She sat down, put her plate down clumsily and picked up the slim parcel. She waved it at Aubrey and then gave a look to Oscar (though what she wanted it to convey, she wasn't sure).

"I mentioned I was feeling cold, oh, weeks ago," she said, "and Aubrey has given me a number of... thoughtful gifts."

"He's a very thoughtful person, isn't he?" said Denise.

"I wonder what it could be this time," she said and began to rip the packaging.

"I —" began Aubrey but she held a hand up to silence him.

"Do not spoil the surprise. A scarf. Electronic handwarmers. Oh! Mittens!"

The package contained a pair of purple, hand-knitted mittens. They looked thick and warm, if clearly a size or two too large for Penny's hands.

"Very nice!" said Penny tartly. "May I suggest that this brings the Cold Penny gift-giving to an end?"

"Um. I didn't give you those," said Aubrey.

Penny stared at them. "Well, of course you did. I told you I was cold. You took it absolutely literally and have inundated me with gifts."

"Three gifts."

"Four!"

"Not those," said Aubrey.

"I recognise the paper, Aubrey. Don't make it weird now because..."

She trailed off, realisation suddenly hitting her. There was of course one other person who had access to this paper.

"Oh, crap," said Penny and immediately shoved the mittens under herself and sat on them.

"Are you now making it weird?" Oscar whispered to her.

"What's going on?" said Izzy, returning with Marcin to the table.

Penny looked at her and pulled a pained expression. "I'm sorry, I..." She put the ripped present on the table.

Izzy's mouth formed around a question.

"Nice mittens!" said Marcin.

"I saw the paper," said Penny, "which you saved from the last present, right?"

"Why did you open Marcin's present?" said Izzy.

"They're for me?" said Marcin, delighted with this development.

"You put them on my seat," said Penny.

"I did not."

"They were here and..."

Izzy's face switched from place to place. "No, I..." She pointed. "Hang on. Someone moved."

"Do I get my mittens now?" said Marcin.

"You moved," Izzy said to Tyrone.

"Wonky seat, so I shifted round one," said the lorry driver apologetically.

"Such a thoughtful gift," said Marcin.

"Thoughtful, yes," said Aubrey who seemed to think that thoughtfulness was under attack.

"Nice shade of purple," agreed Oscar.

"Well, if our haulage friend here sat there," said Denise. "Then I guess I just took the next seat round and then..."

Penny pointed at Aubrey at Oscar and herself. "So, you left it on Marcin's seat but by the time everyone came back, we'd shuffled round and... I'm sorry, Marcin. Sorry, Izzy."

Aubrey cleared his throat.

"Fine," Penny tutted. "Sorry, Aubrey."

Marcin took the mittens. "Very soft. I lost my last ones when out husky sledding."

An unbidden thought descended on Penny. "What if... what if that's why the murderer killed Cat."

Tyrone nearly choked on a prawn. "Who killed what now?"

Denise drew lines between four of them. "We've all been recently asking questions about a friend's murder."

"I have not," said Marcin. "I just train dogs."

"I just sell high quality fabrics," said Oscar. "But what's a pair of mittens got to do with a murder? And did you say husky sledding?"

Izzy looked at Penny as she sat down. Their eyes locked.

"The mittens are Cat in this analogy, right?" said Izzy.

"Er, yes. I guess."

"Cat mittens?" said Tyrone, who had a lot of catching up to do.

Penny swept her hand around the table. "The lodges down the hill are arranged in a circle, a little like us at this table. Six lodges, even though there are seven of us here. On the night Cat was murdered, she and Olivia swapped lodges, not unlike the way we've just swapped seats. We've pondered this, always assuming the lodge swap was unimportant or, indeed, that it was a deliberate ploy by the killer."

"This is a real murder?" said Tyrone. "Not something off the telly?"

"People say country life is dull. How wrong they are," said Oscar, topping up the wine glasses around him.

"What if the murderer didn't know Olivia and Cat had

swapped lodges, and they went to Cat's lodge thinking it was Olivia's?"

"Olivia was the target," said Izzy. "We thought Cat and Gavin were the murder victims, but the real targets were Olivia and Gavin?"

"There are two murders now?" said Tyrone.

Penny gestured to the empty spaces at their table. "I think the reason why we have lots of room at this table is because this was where Gavin, Cat and Cat's plus one were supposed to sit."

"The plus one is dead?"

"The plus one is irrelevant."

Aubrey, Oscar and Marcin exchanged silent looks, a confederacy of irrelevant plus ones.

"And what would you do if you planned to surprise someone and ended up surprising yourself because your intended target wasn't the person at the door?" said Izzy. "What did you do when you realised your mistake with the mittens, Penny?"

"I sat on them," said Penny.

"Buried the mistake in concrete," observed Denise soberly.

"Concrete?" said Tyrone.

"I am just treating this as table theatre," said Oscar.

"They fit perfectly," said Marcin, flexing his hands in his new mittens.

Penny was trying to comprehend this new perspective.

"So the killer never meant to kill Cat. We had this all wrong. They meant to kill Olivia but they killed Cat and then Gavin. Is this all about Olivia?"

They looked over to the top table. The top table were all being brought their main courses. James himself brought Olivia's plate. The woman was putting on a truly brave face in the circumstances.

"If Olivia was the intended target and Cat the accidental victim that doesn't leave a long list of suspects," said Denise. "Monica, Briony, Shirley..."

"You," said Izzy pointedly.

"And you," said Denise back at her.

"Woah, let us not be accusing each other of murders at the dinner table," suggested Marcin.

"Hear, hear," said Aubrey.

"Perhaps we keep the conversation light and non-murderous for the remainder of the dinner?" suggested Oscar.

Penny puffed out her cheeks. "Quite. It's our turn to get our main courses."

44

Even if it wasn't hand-delivered, the food was delicious, and the buffet-style approach gave Penny a chance to ask for an extra profiterole on her dessert. Oscar declared profiteroles to be a hideous cliché so she ate his too.

There were speeches and, whether or not it was because of the sombre events that hung over the wedding, the speeches were short and avoided much of the usual ribaldry of wedding speeches. Conversely, throughout them all, no mention was made of the murder victims. Penny sensed Shirley's hand in this; no mother wanted murder mentioned on her daughter's wedding day.

The cake, superbly finished by the staff at Wallerton's cake shop, was wheeled out and cut, and then two tables were moved so that a dance floor could be created. The newlyweds had their first dance and Oscar approved of the fact that they had not indulged in a carefully choreographed performance dance.

"How should dances be?" Penny asked.

"Impromptu," he said. "Awkwardly amateurish." He took her hand. "Intimate."

"Oh. Oh, really?"

She smiled and, when the playlist shifted to a disco number, she allowed herself to be pulled to the dance floor. Oscar actually had some moves on him. He was a slender man and when the music played it was like he had joints made of rubber. He wriggled and jived around her. His manner was deliberately ridiculous and made Penny laugh but she could instantly tell this guy had a natural and rather sexy rhythm.

She glanced across and saw Denise and Aubrey on the dance floor. Aubrey definitely had been to the school of 'dad dancing'. Sure, he could move in time to the beat, but his moves were self-conscious and from another decade entirely.

"You and, er, Aubrey…" said Oscar, slowing his dance into a gentle sway.

Penny felt the blood drain from her face and looked Oscar in the eye.

"I am so sorry," she said.

He laughed at that, which was unexpected.

"You had a thing?" he said.

"No, no," she said. "Maybe he thought we had a thing. Or we both did. I…"

He took hold of her arms gently. "I don't have a right to interrogate your personal life. This is just a… a date?"

"I'd like to think it is."

The music had changed, softened. She hadn't noticed it do that. They were close together now, his hands on her shoulders, her hands on his waist. He leaned close.

"May I?"

She answered by leaning to meet him, and kissed him. Her first thought wasn't exactly that it had been a long time since she'd kissed someone like that, but it seemed like a long-closed doorway to a long corridor had been opened at last, and she found herself falling headlong into it.

When they broke, he was smiling.

"I've been waiting to do that for a long time," he said.

"You've been sweet on me for a while?"

"I wouldn't put it like that," he grinned. The comment struck a chord in her but she couldn't recall why. She pushed it from her mind.

She leaned forward to kiss Oscar again, but this time he held back.

"I need to tell you something," he said.

"Oh?"

"Meant to tell you some time ago. On the phone, last time we chatted. Remember, I was with a friend..."

He sounded serious, and a coldness crept into the edges of her happy mood.

"You're in relationship with Emily the beautiful fashion designer."

He laughed out loud. "That was your first thought?"

"I... I don't know. It just popped into my head."

"For one, Emily is twice my age. Two, she's in a committed relationship with a cockapoo called Bruno. Three, there's only one woman I'm interested in."

"Me?"

"You!"

"Okay, so what is it? You're dying. You've been living a lie. You're moving away. You're secretly a wanted international assassin."

"Yes."

"You're an international assassin?"

"Um. No. Not that one. Although I do think I could cut a dashing figure in a tux at some post-modernist supervillain lair."

"I think you have a loose concept of what international assassins actually do." She frowned. "You're leaving."

His mouth tightened. "You know Emily the fashion designer —"

"In a committed relationship with a cockapoo."

"— who was trying to sell me on the idea of a job in New York that clearly didn't exist."

"Yes?"

Oscar sighed. "Turns out the job does exist after all, and I've been offered it."

Penny blinked. "You... you are going to work in New York?"

"Leaving next weekend. That fabric company in the garment district. I believe the phrase is they like my 'moxie'."

"Chutzpah," she said.

"That too."

She didn't know what to say. Inside, she was feeling suddenly numb.

"That's... That's wonderful news," she managed to say and kissed him with a fresh fierceness.

"It's come at a rotten time," he said. "This…"

"This is just a date, right?" she said. "But how are you going to help me with crazy dress commissions if you're in completely the wrong time zone?" she managed to add before bursting into tears.

He held her close, arms wrapped around her. She pressed her face into his shoulder, tried to avoid automatically wiping her nose on his lapel, and then she put a kiss on his cheek.

"I might have had one too many glasses of wine," she said.

"We could have some more," he suggested. "And toast futures?"

"Futures plural?"

"Ones that will happen and ones that won't?"

"And some that still might yet happen," she said.

"That's the spirit."

He whipped out a handkerchief and she dabbed her eyes.

"Wine," she agreed.

45

After an hour on the dance floor and a very energetic dance to the Macarena, Izzy and Marcin retired to the table in need of refreshments. Winter days were short and, beyond the huge windows of the orangery, the snowy world was already beginning to darken. Her cousin Olivia was sitting there with Denise and Aubrey.

Events manager James came over with a bottle of fizz in an ice bucket in one hand and a silver platter containing a pot of tea and cups in the other.

"Extra beverages for those who need them," he said and placed the tea tray within Olivia's easy reach.

"What would I do without you?" she said.

"I have no idea," he said.

Penny and Oscar returned to the table and, to Izzy's eyes, it seemed that Penny was clutching his hand too tightly, as though she feared he might evaporate at any moment.

"I've absolutely no clue how any of us are going to get home again," said Aubrey. "That snow is just piling on."

"Might get Monica to bring over a fleet of Land Rovers to assist us," suggested Penny.

"Or we could just stay for the night," said Denise and gave Aubrey a cheeky look.

Monica drifted over with Briony and Ross who were doing their wedding duty of checking in and chatting with all of the guests.

"Your feller there going to wear those all night?" asked Monica, pointing at Marcin's new purple mittens.

"They are very cosy," Marcin said in his defence.

Briony flopped into a seat with a very loud and squeaky 'oof' of exhaustion. It was possible the bride had relied on quite a lot of alcoholic sustenance to get her through the day. She lifted a slightly unsteady hand and stroked the head of Monica's swan.

"This really is lovely," she said and then flung her hands out wide. "All of this is very lovely."

"I believe we said as much earlier," said Denise.

"The word lovely was used a lot," Oscar agreed.

"All my favourite people gathered together, just like my..." She stopped. Izzy knew she was about to say 'my hen night' but had halted herself before stepping into those tragic memories.

She looked at the small bouquet she had been carrying for much of the day.

"They usually do a bouquet toss, don't they? But I just wanted to..." She passed the bouquet to Olivia. "We all love you, Olivia, and are so glad you're here with us."

Olivia, who had been doing a surprisingly good job of holding it together throughout the day, took the flowers and looked at them with hollow, emotionally shattered eyes.

People often did not know how to act in proximity to death, and Izzy could see a taut embarrassment in the eyes of some. From Olivia's other side, Denise put a hand on Olivia's arm.

"Gavin would have loved today," she said. "He was a great guy, wasn't he?"

"He was my perfect man," said Olivia. "I'll never..."

It was too much for Olivia, and the tears began to flow. Out of nowhere, James appeared with a napkin for her, and she pressed it against her crying eyes.

Izzy felt a rumbling within herself. It wasn't a physical rumbling, nor was it audible. The rumbling was in her mind, in the core of herself. She wondered briefly if she'd danced too hard and her tummy, full of prawn cocktail, roast dinner and sticky profiteroles was about to violently protest. But, no, the disturbance was in her mind, in her eyes, the spinning lurch of seeing an optical illusion for what it was, the rollercoaster plunge of realising she had been lied to.

She looked at Penny and Penny met her gaze. Maybe Penny could see the rising, rumbling tide inside Izzy because Penny's face took on a warning expression. Or maybe Penny had felt it too.

The words came to Izzy before she had chance to stop them.

"No, he wasn't," she said.

Faces turned her way.

"He wasn't your perfect man," she said to Olivia. "Not at

all. And he wouldn't have liked it here today. He'd have hated it. Gavin hated parties. He never came to Nanna Lem's eightieth last year and he'd probably have found an excuse to not come today."

"Steady on," said Monica, surprised.

"You can't start badmouthing a man because he's dead," said Denise. "He might not have been perfect, but he was perfect for Olivia. Have a heart."

"Except he wasn't," said Izzy. "On the night Cat died, Olivia said exactly that. She said…" She closed her eyes and tried to remember. "You said that 'only the other day' you said you wanted a man who would be crazy about you and couldn't live without you. You wanted a man to come swooping in."

"The man from Del Monte," said Shirley, nodding, as she approached the table. "What are we talking about?"

"Wrong advert. She means the Milk Tray man," said Denise.

"Swooping in with a box of chocolates," added Penny, and Izzy saw a glimmer of understanding on her face.

"Just because she said that, doesn't mean she meant it," Briony tutted. "We were all slagging off our other halves."

"Were you?" asked Ross.

"Not you, love," she said blithely and patted his hand.

"But sometimes we hear things and take them to heart," said Izzy.

"Like when I tell someone that my room is a bit cold," Penny said pointedly to Aubrey.

"This again?" he said. "I was just trying to be nice to a… a friend."

"Because we want to please the ones we love," Izzy agreed. "We want the ones we love to see us for who we are." She took a deep breath. "I know who killed Cat."

Penny nodded in firm agreement. "So do I. The person who killed Gavin, too."

Olivia, napkin in hand, dabbed a final tear from her eyes and stared at the two of them.

"You two know who killed them?" said Monica. "Why would you two know?"

"It's not very difficult to grasp it when you see it," said Penny.

"We were working on the assumption that the person who killed Cat must have already been down by the lodges, because you can't come between them and the house without setting off the security lights," said Izzy. "And who had we seen all evening except each other?"

She looked round at Shirley, Monica, Briony, Olivia and Denise.

"We all had reasons to hate Cat," she said, and when Shirley opened her mouth to protest, Izzy doubled down. "We did, Shirley! Maybe not to kill her, but we had all experienced Cat's selfishness. And so Penny and I were focussed on those motives."

"Focussed?" sneered Shirley. "Clearly there's not enough work in your little sewing shop to keep your minds occupied."

"We only looked at what we thought we were supposed to look at," said Penny. She gestured across to the dance floor, where Tyrone the lorry driver was boogying down with a gaggle of hyperactive children.

"Tyrone got his dinner before all of us. Just sauntered to the front and pretended he belonged here."

"Silent men in the background," said Izzy. She looked at Ross and Aubrey and Oscar. "Dependable, solid presences. Loved but overlooked."

"Irrelevant *and* overlooked," noted Oscar without rancour.

"It's like today," Izzy laughed. "Until he got in the car, Briony, I forgot you had a dad. Your mum does talking enough for both."

"Well, really!" said Shirley.

"That's just the way of things," said Penny.

"And I know you love Mr Hart," said Izzy. "To hear you two tell the story of how you met. You running into the back of his car deliberately to strike up a conversation."

"Not wholly unlike the story of how Olivia and Gavin became a couple," said Penny.

"What on earth has that got to do with anything?" asked Olivia.

"Everything," said Penny. "It is absolutely everything. Briony broke her leg. You asked your good friend, James, to go with Briony to the hospital and you presented yourself to Gavin as 'a shoulder to cry on in the aftermath of a tragedy'. That's how you make someone love you."

"Are you saying this is my fault?" Olivia's brow was creased in anger and confusion. "Do you know or do you not know who killed Gavin?"

"We do," said Izzy, standing.

"Words," said Penny, also standing. "It's all words. It's what happens when we take people's words and we accidentally or deliberately misunderstand them. I had a moment out there on the dance floor." She gripped Oscar's shoulder. "I've just found and lost this wonderful man, and while we were there on the dance floor I said to him 'You've been sweet on me for a while.' I didn't realise it, but I was quoting something I'd heard before. We do that. We pick up phrases we hear and spit them back out. I told him he'd been sweet on me and he said to me that he 'wouldn't put it like that.'"

"I wouldn't," agreed Oscar. "Sweet on someone. Ugh. It's an undercooked phrase."

"Right. A belittling phrase," said Penny. "Because when he said he wouldn't put it like that, I could have taken it to mean that he wasn't sweet on me at all. I could have and I would have been wrong, just as it would have been wrong the last time you had it said to you, Olivia."

"Me?" said Olivia.

"Penny and I have deduced that this whole affair — these murders — it's all about you, Olivia," said Izzy. "I'm sorry, but it is."

"Olivia did it?" asked Denise.

"No, of course, she didn't," said Izzy. "Move a body through the woods in the dark and know where the boats are and then push her corpse down into the concrete? She's practically a twig. Can't lift anything."

"Cat's killer came to that lodge thinking that it was Olivia in there. *Knowing* it was Olivia in there, because that was the lodge she'd been given. But why did the killer go there? What did you find on the grass behind the lodges, Aubrey?" said Penny.

"A box of vegan chocolates."

"The Milk Tray man?" said Shirley.

"How could anyone have approached the lodges without activating the lights? It's impossible," said Penny, and swung a finger in the general direction of the hotel reception. "Unless, of course, they just turned them off from reception."

"And what would that person do if they broke into a lodge and surprised the wrong woman?" added Izzy. "How would Cat have reacted?"

"She would have probably been mean about it as soon as she realised what was going on. I can almost hear her laughing in his face, saying that even a dullard like Olivia wouldn't be interested. So then he hits her on the head with something close to hand, and then tries to hide the evidence of the dead body," said Penny. "And if your first attempt to get close to the object of your affection has failed, then what might you do?"

Izzy gave a sad smile. "Be the shoulder to cry on when tragedy strikes. And if there is no tragedy to hand, you might just have to create one."

"Gavin?" said Olivia. "You're saying that Gavin was killed in…"

"In order to make you sad and weak and vulnerable," Izzy nodded. "And, of course, to get your potential husband-to-be out of the way."

Penny turned to James. "You've been sweet on Olivia for quite a while now, haven't you?"

The hotel events manager's eyes went wide for a second in momentary panic.

"I..." he began, and then swallowed. "I wouldn't put it quite like that."

"James?" said Olivia. "He's not in love with me. He's just... just..."

"Exactly," said Penny. "He's just that man in the background. A friend. Ever since we were at school together. I couldn't put a name to his face when I met him again the other day. What a terrible punishment, to always be there but never seen. The kind of trait that perhaps only comes in handy when you're trying to get away with murder. You wanted a man to make a dramatic gesture and declare his love for you. You wanted a shoulder to cry on. James obliged."

James' chest was rising and falling rapidly, like he was trying to stop himself hyperventilating.

"You can't prove it," he said.

"Really?" said Izzy. "Because I bet there's a wedge shoe in a bin somewhere with your fingerprints on it. Or maybe a terracotta pot in Gavin's shop."

"There will be that one clue. Somewhere," added Penny.

James became very still.

"So, what happens now?" he said.

"Maybe you should go to reception and call the police yourself," suggested Izzy.

"I've got some cracking video footage to show them," said Monica, tapping the eyepiece of her swan costume.

James nodded numbly and moved off before hesitating and turning back.

"I... I sometimes fall into the trap of doing what I think I should be doing rather than what I want to be doing." The look on his long, funereal face was that of a man crestfallen, destroyed. "And this is what happens when I finally do what I want."

He walked away and while he was still in sight, no one at the table said a word.

46

The lights of the police cars were visible from over a mile away.

Blue light shone in the crisp evening air and reflected off the luminescent snow that lay in a thick blanket over Suffolk. James Coombes, not even bothering to put a coat on, had walked down the driveway to meet them.

Penny and Oscar stood on the steps of Letheringham Hall and watched him disappear into the gloom.

"So," said Oscar, "James came down to what he thought was Olivia's lodge with a box of chocolates with the intention of — what? — professing his love for her and sweeping her off her feet?"

Penny chuckled humourlessly. "If you've loved someone from afar for — well, not even from afar. If you've loved your best friend for all your adult life, then maybe any action seems reasonable."

"And then, when that didn't work, he decided to bump off

her existing boyfriend so he could be there to pick up the pieces afterwards?"

"He was there right outside the shop with Izzy waiting for Olivia to turn up, literally ready with his shoulder for her to cry on."

"Insane."

"Actually, that part of the plot might even have worked. Assuming the police didn't bumble their way to him eventually. We make big decisions at weak moments."

"Love makes us crazy," said Oscar. "It destroys us."

Penny breathed in deeply and realised it was very cold. She offered her arm to Oscar and steered him back into the hotel building.

"New York is going to love you," she said.

He sighed. "I could tell them no."

"Don't you bloody dare, Oscar Connelly. You will go there and you will be amazing and, maybe, I will come over at some point for a holiday and you can show me the New York garment district."

"I would love that."

She hugged his arm to her side and thought about the months she had known him and the months they had wasted in not getting to know each other better. But she could curse her own stupidity at her leisure.

Most of the guests were still enjoying the wedding dance. Few had any inclination to go anywhere in this weather. Penny looked for Olivia but couldn't see her. The woman would have a lot to process. There was no Briony in sight either, so perhaps the friends were together somewhere.

On the dance floor, a soppy eighties power ballad was

playing and happy couples were swaying in each other's arms. Denise had Aubrey in a tight embrace. He said something, inaudible over the music, and Denise laughed. Not far off, Izzy and Marcin were dancing, twirling each other around with no regard for how silly they looked.

"Love isn't insane," said Penny. "Love doesn't destroy. It's people that do that."

She smiled to see Marcin was still wearing his purple knitted mittens.

"Love is wonderful, don't you think?" she said.

ABOUT THE AUTHOR

Millie Ravensworth writes the Cozy Craft series of books. Her love of murder mysteries and passion for dressmaking made her want to write books full of quirky characters and unbelievable murders.

Millie lives in central England where children and pets are something of a distraction from the serious business of writing, although dog walking is always a good time to plot the next book.